Nostalgic Blood

7/28/22

D0401870

by

J. CROCKETT

Full Definition of *NOSTALGIA*

1

: the state of being homesick : <u>homesickness</u>

2

: a <u>wistful</u> or excessively sentimental yearning for return to or of some past period or irrecoverable condition; *also* : something that evokes nostalgia

nostalgic

adjective <u>sentimental</u>, <u>longing</u>, <u>emotional</u>, <u>homesick</u>, <u>wistful</u>, <u>maudlin</u>, <u>regretful</u> I got nostalgic the other night and dug out my old photos.

Blood in this novel represent familyBloodline definitionYour *bloodline* is your heritage or ancestry. In other words, your *bloodline* includes your parents, grandparents, great-grandparents, and so on.

The Old English root word *blod*, means "blood." By the 13th century, *blood* also meant "family" or "heritage."

Acknowledgements

-

     No one walks alone on the journey of life. Just where do you start to thank those that joined you, walked beside you, and helped you along the way continuously urged me to write a book, to put my thoughts down on over the years, those that I have met and worked with have paper, and to share my insights together with the secrets to my continual, positive approach to life and all that life throws at us. So at last, here it is. So, perhaps this book and its pages will be seen as "thanks" to the tens of thousands of you who have helped make my life what is today. Much of what I have learned over the years will be identified as you read this book. Some of your names had to be changed, but I am sure that you guys would understand. Many of you have inspired me and, subconsciously contributed a tremendous amount to the content of this book. A little bit of each of them will be found here weaving in and out of the pages – in loving memory for those who did not make it out alive. I also have to thank Roseanne Beam for being supportive, motivating, and pushing me beyond description, which I can't say. I also need to thank my mom Annie Copeland, a wonderful woman who kept me under her wing; any time my mind strayed I thought about how she would feel. My stepdad Andy Copeland for being a guide in my life. My dad, Joseph Crockett thank you for being so honest about life in general. You saved me in many ways. Even though you don't think my book will do well, time will tell.

-      It's strange to think that I have been working on this book for 20 years. I lost it three times, recovered it somehow through the grace of the higher power; I believe it was meant for me to complete this book and share my story with the world. Valencia Copeland, I can't thank you enough for everything you have done. Vivian Copeland, keep inventing because it's worth it. I also want to thank all of you who took the time out of your day to help with the book cover survey, thanks, guys. That helped me.

-      I want to thank Custom Plastic and signs, Chris Cuevas for being so patient with me with designing the book cover. I know I can be picky, if not for your expertise, who knows what the book cover would look like. For any printing of signs, plastic moldings, Chris can do it. Call him 209 933 9711

-

- Lyrell   McGee, thanks for everything you did, just did not have enough time, when you are ready to publish, I will be there for you.

- Last but not least, I want to thank all of the Stocktonians who took a   chance and bought my book. Some of you gave me whatever you had as a donation to help me climb to the level of publishing. It was you, the residents of Stockton, Ca that helped me get into the stores worldwide. Thank you so much. Look forward to more great books from me.

History of North Korea from Wikipedia

North Korea (listen), officially the**Democratic People's Republic of Korea**(**DPRK**; Chosŏn'gŭl: 조선민주주의인민공화국;hancha: 朝鮮民主主義人民共和國;MR: *Chosŏn Minjujuŭi Inmin Konghwaguk*), is a country in East Asia, in the northern part of the Korean Peninsula. The name *Korea* is derived from the Kingdom of Goryeo, also spelled as *Koryŏ*. The capital and largest city is Pyongyang. North Korea shares a land border with China to the north and north-west, along the Amnok (Yalu) and Tumen rivers, and a small section of the Tumen River also forms a border with Russia to the north-east.[8] The Korean Demilitarized Zone marks the *de facto* boundary between North Korea and South Korea. The legitimacy of this border is not accepted by either side, as both states claim to be the legitimate government of the entire peninsula.

The Empire of Japan annexed Korea in 1910. After the Japanese surrender at the end ofWorld War II in 1945, Korea was divided into two zones by the United States and the Soviet Union, with the north occupied by the Sovietsand the south by the Americans. Negotiations on reunification failed, and in 1948 two separate governments were formed: the Democratic People's Republic of Korea in the north, and the Republic of Korea in the south.

These conflicting claims of sovereignty led to the Korean War (1950–53). Although the Korean Armistice Agreement brought about a ceasefire, no official peace treaty was ever signed.[9] Both states were accepted into the United Nations in 1991.[10]

The DPRK officially describes itself as a self-reliant socialist state and holds elections.[11]Internationally, however, it is considered a totalitarian dictatorship. Various

outlets have called it Stalinist,[20][21][22] particularly noting the elaborate cult of personality around Kim Il-sung and his family. International organizations have also assessed human rights violations in North Korea as

belonging to a category of their own, with no parallel in the contemporary world.[23][24][25] The Workers' Party of Korea, led by a member of the ruling family,[22] holds power in the state and leads the Democratic Front for the Reunification of the Fatherland of which all political officers are required to be a member.[26]

Over time North Korea has gradually distanced itself from the world communist movement. *Juche*, an ideology of national self-reliance, was introduced into the constitution as a "creative application of Marxism–Leninism" in 1972.[27][28] The means of production are owned by the state through state-run enterprises and collectivized farms. Most services such as healthcare, education, housing and food production are subsidized or state-funded.[29]In the late 1990s, North Korea suffered from a famine that resulted in the deaths of hundreds of thousands of civilians; the country continues to struggle with food production.[30]

North Korea follows *Songun*, or "military-first" policy.[31] It is the world's most militarized society, with a total of 9,495,000 active, reserve, and paramilitary personnel[*citation needed*]. Its active duty army of 1.21 million is the fourth largest in the world, after China, the U.S., and India.[32] It also possesses nuclear weapons.[33][34]

Nostalgic Blood takes place during the Kim Jong Il dictatorship, from biography.com is his life story.

Kim Jong Il's dominating personality and complete concentration of power has come to define the country North Korea. Born in either 1941 or 1942, much of Kim Jong Il's persona is based on a cult of personality, meaning that legend and official North Korean government accounts describe his life, character, and actions in ways that promote and legitimize his leadership, including his birth. Over the years, Kim's dominating personality and complete concentration of power have come to define the country of North Korea.

Early Life

Born February 16, 1941, though official accounts place birth a year later. Some mystery surrounds when and where Kim Jong Il was born. Official North Korean biographies state that his birth occurred on February 16, 1942, in a secret camp on Mount Paekdu along the Chinese border, in Samjiyon County, Ryanggang Province, in the Democratic People's Republic of Korea (North Korea). Other reports indicate he was born a year later in Vyatskoye in the former Soviet Union.

During World War II, his father commanded the 1st Battalion of the Soviet 88th Brigade, composed of Chinese and Korean exiles battling the Japanese Army. Kim Jong Il's mother was Kim Jong Suk, his father's first wife. Official accounts indicate that Kim Jong Il comes from a family of nationalists who actively resisted imperialism from the Japanese in the early 20th century.

His official government biography claims Kim Jong Il completed his general education between September 1950 and August 1960 in Pyongyang, the current capital city of North Korea. But scholars point out that the first few years of this period were during the Korean War and contend his early education took place in the People's Republic of China, where it was safer to live. Official accounts claim that throughout his schooling, Kim was involved in politics. While attending the Namsan Higher Middle School in Pyongyang, he was active in the Children's Union—a youth organization that promotes the concept of Juche, or the spirit of self-reliance—and the Democratic Youth League (DYL), taking part in the study of Marxist political theory. During his youth, Kim Jong Il showed an interest in a wide range of subjects including agriculture, music, and mechanics. In high school, he took classes in automotive repair and participated in trips to farms and factories. Official accounts of his early schooling also point out his leadership capabilities: as vice chairman of his school's DYL branch, he encouraged younger classmates to pursue greater ideological education and organized academic competitions and seminars as well as field trips.

Kim Jong Il graduated from Namsan Higher Middle School in 1960 and enrolled the same year in Kim Il Sung University. He majored in Marxist political economy and minored in philosophy and military science. While at the university, Kim trained as an apprentice in a textile machine factory and took classes in building TV broadcast equipment. During this time, he also accompanied his father on tours of field guidance in several of North Korea's provinces.

Rise to Power

Kim Jong Il joined the Workers' Party, the official ruling party of North Korea, in July 1961. Most political experts believe the party follows the traditions of Stalinist politics even though North Korea began distancing itself from Soviet domination in 1956. The Workers' Party claims to have its own ideology, steeped in the philosophy of Juche. However, in the late 1960s, the party instituted a policy of "burning loyalty" to the "Great Leader" (Kim Il Sung). This practice of personality cult is reminiscent of Stalinist Russia but was taken to new heights with Kim Il Sung and would continue with Kim Jong Il.

Soon after his 1964 graduation from the university, Kim Jong Il began his rise through the ranks of the Korean Workers' Party. The 1960s were a time of high tension between many Communist countries. China and the Soviet Union were clashing over ideological differences that resulted in several border skirmishes, Soviet satellite nations in Eastern Europe were simmering with dissention, and North Korea was pulling away from both Soviet and Chinese influence. Within North Korea, internal forces were attempting to revise the party's revolutionary message. Kim Jong Il was appointed to the Workers' Party Central Committee to lead the offensive against the revisionists and ensure the party did not deviate from the ideological line set by his father. He also led efforts to expose dissidents and deviant policies to ensure strict enforcement of the party's ideological system. In addition, he took on major military reform to strengthen the party's control of the military and expelled disloyal officers.

Kim Jong Il oversaw the Propaganda and Agitation Department, the government agency responsible for media control and censorship. Kim gave firm instructions that the party's monolithic ideological message be communicated constantly by writers, artists, and officials in the media. According to official accounts, he revolutionized Korean fine arts by encouraging the production of new works in new media. This included the art of film and cinema. Mixing history, political ideology, and movie-making, Kim encouraged the production of several epic films, which glorified works written by his father. His official biography claims that Kim Jong Il has composed six operas and enjoys staging elaborate musicals. Kim is reported to be an avid film buff who owns more than 20,000 movies, including the entire series of James Bond films, for his personal enjoyment.

Kim Il Sung began preparing his son to lead North Korea in the early 1970s. Between 1971 and 1980, Kim Jong Il was appointed to increasingly important positions in the Korean Workers' Party. During this time, he instituted policies to bring party officials closer to the people by forcing bureaucrats to work among subordinates for one month a year. He launched the Three-Revolution Team Movement, in which teams of political, technical, and scientific technicians traveled around the country to provide training. He was also involved in economic planning to develop certain sectors of the economy.

By the 1980s, preparations were being made for Kim to succeed his father as the leader of North Korea. At this time, the government began building a personality cult around Kim Jong Il patterned after that of his father. Just as Kim Il Sung was known as the "Great Leader," Kim Jong Il was hailed in the North Korean media as the "fearless leader" and "the great successor to the revolutionary cause." His portraits appeared in public buildings along with his father's. He also initiated a series of drop-in inspections of businesses, factories, and government offices. At the Sixth Party Congress in 1980, Kim Jong Il was given senior posts in the Politburo (the policy committee of the Korean Workers' Party), the Military Commission, and the Secretariat (the executive department charged with carrying out policy). Thus, Kim was positioned to control all aspects of the government.

The one area of leadership in which Kim Jong Il might have had a perceived weakness was the military. The army was the foundation of power in North Korea, and Kim had no military service experience. With the assistance of allies in the military, Kim was able to gain acceptance by the army officials as the next leader of North Korea. By 1991, he was designated as the supreme commander of the Korean People's Army, thus giving him the tool he needed to maintain complete control of the government once he took power.

Following the death of Kim Il Sung in July 1994, Kim Jong Il took total control of the country. This transition of power from father to son had never been seen before in a communist regime. In deference to his father, the office of president was abolished, and Kim Jong Il took the titles of general secretary of the

Workers' Party and chairman of the National Defense Commission, which was declared the highest office of the state.

Foreign Aid and Nuclear Testing

It is important to understand that much of Kim Jong Il's persona is based on a cult of personality, meaning that legend and official North Korean government accounts describe his life, character, and actions in ways that promote and legitimize his leadership. Examples include his family's nationalist revolutionary roots and claims that his birth was foretold by a swallow, the appearance of a double rainbow over Mount Paekdu, and a new star in the heavens. He is known to personally manage the country's affairs and set operational guidelines for individual industries. He is said to be arrogant and self-centered in policy decisions, openly rejecting criticism or opinions that differ from his. He is suspicious of nearly all of those who surround him and volatile in his emotions. There are many stories of his eccentricities, his playboy lifestyle, the lifts in his shoes and pompadour hairstyle that make him appear taller, and his fear of flying. Some stories can be verified while others are most likely exaggerated, possibly circulated by foreign operatives from hostile countries.

In the 1990s, North Korea went through a series of devastating and debilitating economic episodes. With the collapse of the Soviet Union in 1991, North Korea lost its main trading partner. Strained relations with China following China's normalization with South Korea in 1992 further limited North Korea's trade options. Record-breaking floods in 1995 and 1996 followed by drought in 1997 crippled North Korea's food production. With only 18 percent of its land suitable for farming in the best of times, North Korea began experiencing a devastating famine. Worried about his position in power, Kim Jong Il instituted the Military First policy, which prioritized national resources to the military. Thus, the military would be pacified and remain in his control. Kim could defend himself from threats domestic and foreign, while economic conditions worsened. The policy did produce some economic growth and along with some socialist-type market practices—characterized as a "flirtation with capitalism"—North Korea has been able to remain operational despite being heavily dependent on foreign aid for food.

In 1994, the Clinton administration and North Korea agreed to a framework designed to freeze and eventually dismantle North Korea's nuclear weapons program. In exchange, the United States would provide assistance in producing two power-generating nuclear reactors and supplying fuel oil and other economic aid. In 2000, the presidents of North Korea and South Korea met for diplomatic talks and agreed to promote reconciliation and economic cooperation between the two countries. The agreement allowed families from both countries to reunite and signaled a move toward increased trade and investment. For a time, it appeared that North Korea was reentering the international community.

Then in 2002, U.S. intelligence agencies suspected North Korea was enriching uranium or building the facilities to do so, presumably for making nuclear weapons. In his 2002 State of the Union address, President George W. Bush identified North Korea as one of the countries in the "axis of evil" (along with Iraq and Iran). The Bush administration soon revoked the 1994 treaty designed to eliminate North Korea's nuclear weapons program. Finally, in 2003, Kim Jong Il's government admitted to having produced nuclear weapons for security purposes, citing tensions with President Bush. Late in 2003, the Central Intelligence Agency issued a report that North Korea possessed one and possibly two nuclear bombs. The Chinese government stepped in to try to mediate a settlement, but President Bush refused to meet with Kim Jong Il one-on-one and instead insisted on multilateral negotiations. China was able to gather Russia, Japan, South Korea, and the United States for negotiations with North Korea. Talks were held in 2003, 2004, and twice in 2005. All through the meetings, the Bush administration demanded North Korea eliminate its nuclear weapons program. It adamantly maintained any normalcy of relations between North Korea and the United States would come about only if North Korea changed its human rights policies, eliminated all chemical and biological weapons programs, and ended missile technology proliferation. North Korea continually rejected the proposal. In 2006, North Korea's Central News Agency announced North Korea had successfully conducted an underground nuclear bomb test.

Failing Health

There have been many reports and claims regarding Kim Jong Il's health and physical condition. In August 2008, a Japanese publication claimed Kim had died in 2003 and had been replaced with a stand-in for public appearances. It was also noted that Kim hadn't made a public appearance for the Olympic torch ceremony in Pyongyang in April 2008. After Kim failed to show up for a military parade celebrating North Korea's 60th anniversary, U.S. intelligence agencies believed Kim to be gravely ill after possibly suffering a stroke. During the fall of 2008, numerous news sources gave conflicting reports on his condition. The North Korean news agency reported Kim participated in national elections in March 2009 and was unanimously elected to a seat in the Supreme People's Assembly, the North Korean parliament. The assembly will vote later to confirm him as chairman of the National Defense Commission. In the report, it was said Kim cast his ballot at the Kim Il Sung University and later toured the facility and talked to a small group of people.

Kim's health was watched closely by other countries because of his volatile nature, the country's possession of nuclear weapons, and its precarious economic condition. Kim also had no apparent successors to his regime, as did his father. His three sons spent most of their lives outside the country and none seemed to be in the favor of the "Dear Leader" to ascend to the top spot. Many international experts believed that when Kim died, there would be mayhem because there seemed to be no apparent method for a transfer of power. But due to the North Korean government's predilection for secrecy, this was too hard to know.

In 2009, however, news reports revealed that Kim planned to name his son, Kim Jong Un as his successor. Very little was known about Kim's heir apparent; until 2010, only one officially confirmed photo of Jong Un existed, and not even his official birthdate had been revealed. The twenty-something was officially confirmed in September 2010.

Kim Jon-Il died December 17, 2011, of a heart attack while traveling on a train. Media reports say the leader was on a work trip for official duties. Upon news of The Dear Leader's death, North Koreans marched on the capital, weeping and mourning.

Kim is said to be survived by three wives, three sons and three daughters. Other reports claim he has fathered 70 children, most of whom are housed in villas throughout North Korea.

His son, Kim Jong Un, is reported to take up leadership, and the military pledged to support Jong Un's succession.

Table of Content

Chapter One

Honolulu, Hawaii

The early morning breeze pushed the lingering fog from the night before through the jogging path. Jamie kept her stride, so Ziggy could keep up. She stopped, "Ziggy, come on boy." She tried to coach him, but he had been intrigued by something. He sniffed until he found a trail through a bush. He came out when he heard his name, looked at her with great concern.

"Boy, if you don't bring your rump here." She wiped her sweat, fanned her face, and went to pick him up, but he ran into the bushes. "Oh my God, are you serious?" Frustrated, she went after him, almost having his tail, "When I get my hands on you." She was dirty from the fall to her knees, scratches from the thorny bushes.

He barked, just out of reach of her fingers; it was almost like he was pulling her closer to where he had been. Just on the other side of this huge leaf, she reached in as hard as she could, grabbed him by the tail. "What the hell are you…" she looked up, not far from where she stood, not believing what she was watching. She covered her mouth to prevent her scream from being heard. "No!" she held Ziggy tight, "Please stop!" She wanted to run, but her feet inched closer, her eyes pooled with fear, "Stop! Please don't hurt him."

Before she knew it, she was closer to the men that were beating a man with objects as he hung from a tree, the screams for help quickly went silent when his mouth was stuffed with a white towel. She could not understand how they ignored her plea. From the corner of his eye, he

1

tried to tell her to run. The blood and wounds that puffed his face were unbearable. She woke up from this reoccurring dream, breathing hard, chest pounded like she had been running. She reached over and slammed her palm on the alarm clock that woke her up. She wanted to know why her dreams were so vivid; it was as if she was really there. She sighed, grabbed her cell and noticed three missed calls from her boyfriend, "Damn, I gotta get going." She jumped up, tossed her panties and bra on as she made her way to the restroom. Her cell rang, with her toothbrush in her mouth, "Hello."

"Hey gorgeous, were you sleeping?" he waited in line to pass through customs.

"Matter of fact I was, but I'll meet you at your house" They both ended the call.

* * *

Honolulu International Airport

"Excuse me, sir, can you please accompany me to my office?" A soft voice came from behind. His nerves started to bother him. But it wasn't unusual under these circumstances.

"Well…" He stuttered. "Sure, why not." He spoke with a smile, wiped the perspiration from his forehead, and wondered if they would notice his hands. She looked at his airline ticket.

"Mr. Kalargo Choi, do you have your passport?" The customs agent asked. He held all his emotions under control, just like he had practiced.

"Well certainly. It should be in my carry-on bag, the side

pocket."

He thought to himself and wondered about the consequences. He looked around and saw himself in the reflection. He sighed. "What did I get myself into?"

He saw a small particle on his shoulder, and immediately removed it with his left hand as if it was illegal. He wore Levi's jeans neatly ironed with a blue polo pullover, and a pair of black ostrich ankle-high boots. Mr. Choi stood no more than 5'10, two hundred fifteen pounds. He was a handsome Gambian who is as ebony as jet ink. He was well built physically and mentally due to years of jiu-jitsu martial arts, which was accompanied by a third-degree black belt. At this moment, customs are the only people he feared.

"Mr. Choi, where are you arriving from?" The customs officer asked him.

He responded quickly. "I'm arriving from South Africa." He remembered to not add anything to the conversation between the two.

"Are you a citizen of the United States of America?"

"Yes, I am." He breathed lightly to ease his nerves.

"How long have you been in South Africa?"

He looked mystified for a split second. "No more than a month." He plunged his pinky finger in his left ear.

"Are you transporting any illegal drugs, weapons, or any items that would be contraband?" the customs agent placed his hands on top of his bags.

"No, I'm not." He spoke with confidence.

"Are you carrying a large amount of cash that you have not declared on your customs sheet?" He looked at the ceiling and quickly returned eye contact.

"No, sir."

"Are you bringing back any gifts?"

He shook his head. "No, sir." He removed a tear of sweat with his right pinky finger. At the same time, the customs officer went through his luggage and took out the obvious. They searched carefully, one item at a time.

"What is this?" He asked.

"I'm sorry. I made that myself upon arriving in South Africa. Is that considered a gift?" He frowned.

The officer gave him an innocent pout. He looked at him, "Not really, I guess not. It's mighty small."

"Where do you reside in the U.S.?"

He was daydreaming and did not hear him. "Excuse me, sir, I asked you a question. Where do you live in the U.S.?" He responded, "Honolulu."

"What's your occupation?"

He smiled, "I'm a martial arts instructor, a personal trainer and I own an import/export business."

The officer looked him in the eyes with his passport in his hand, "Welcome back to the U.S, be careful of the heavy snow in the mountains at this time of the year. You may proceed. Pack your clothes." He said with a steady stare.

Kalargo returned the stare and finally relaxed to a mood of safety and comfort. He sighed with a password. "Tell the people who are visiting Hawaii about the snow." He packed his bags.

"Why can't this be any easier?" He was still nervous as hell. He stood in front of a mirror in the airport bathroom and removed all signs of perspiration and guilt. He perfected his gig line up with his belt. Finally, he combed his hair with an Afro pick.

He walked toward the exit with his luggage in tow, pulled out his cell phone, from memory he dialed Na Min's number and waited.

"Yes hello." A female voice responded in fluent Korean.

"Yes, Na Min." The phone went silent for a moment.

"Yes, He'll be right with you."

He walked toward the limo stand. The Hawaiian heat embraced his face like an old friend who had not seen him in years. He could see the afternoon sun hovering over the horizon. He smiled. "Damn, I'm glad to be back."

A voice interrupted him. "Kalargo, how was your trip?"

He laughed with a joyful voice. "Just great, could not be better.

Na Min had a Korean accent when he spoke English. "Where are you now?"

"Waiting for my driver, I should be home in about forty-five minutes."

"Well I'm glad to know you are back and safe, call me later." After a couple more words, they both terminated the line and he placed the phone in his top left pocket. The driver pulled up alongside him, he tossed his bags in the car, and departed Honolulu International airport to get on the Queen Liliuokalani freeway, he pondered his first day he came to Hawaii and most of all, and how he got to South Korea.

At the age of nine, he lived in The Gambia. Unknown to his knowledge, he was in hiding. He and his uncle lived in a shack under a tin roof. They barely ate four complete meals a week. Mugumbi, his uncle, has been taking care of him for the past five years. After he was laid off from the diamond mine, they struggled for weeks until he found work at the docks. He loved ships and saw them as the beast of the sea. Later he found a way out of Africa, a way to riches. As usual

Kalargo was in the streets while his uncle continued to work hard and planned their great escape.

After three years, his plan came to him in the middle of the night. The next morning he woke up with a smile.

"Good morning little one, it's time to open your eyes and smell the sunshine." He literally meant the humidity including the outstanding stench that floated among them like a friend, a dirty friend or worst a flatulent ghost with murderous intentions. They lived in a small-cemented center block efficiency, half kitchen with an outside bathroom. There was one thing that they had in common and it only occurred in the middle of the night, their dreams, and they ended when their eyelids opened and allowed reality to piss in their faces.

"Tipi, it's time to eat, so go ahead and wash your face, he would've added brushing his teeth to the list of things to do but neither owned one." This time he spoke with a little more authority in his voice. The nickname Tipi stuck to Kalargo ever since he was younger. Most of his family had been killed and leaving to get away from the genocide was the last option. But somehow and for a mysterious reason, it was like they followed them. The house bombing nearly killed him. A huge gash on the side of his neck as a reminder.

He lay on the floor between a dirty sheet and blanket. Surprisingly, his eyes flickered to keep out the early morning sunlight. He yawned to get himself started.

"It's early." Neither of them spoke English nor read or write their own language.

"This week…" He said with a smile. "I have big plans for both of us. But you have to promise me…" He bent down beside him on the floor. He lifted his chin to look him directly in his eyes. He licked his thumb to wet it real good, wiped the dried saliva and eye snot from the corners of his face. Hardly awake he sat upright and looked into his uncle's eyes.

"Why are you so happy?" Before he could finish, his uncle spoke.

"Promise me you'll never say a word! One day you and I will be out of here, just wait you'll see."

Kalargo couldn't believe the words that suddenly became melodic.

"Do you promise not to say a word to no one?"

He was so hungry, he would promise anything at this moment, "I promise, but what are you talking about?" He looked like he was begging for food and lost.

"When the time comes, I'll let you know. From this day on, just be happy and don't ask or mention this conversation again." He knew it would be hard to be happy under these conditions, if he had a plan, it must be a good one.

After six months of waiting, He started to wonder. "Uncle…" He began to say with an inquisitive voice. He stood between the doorway of their shack. He leaned with his left hand on his hip. The humidity made him melt like ice cream and his upper lip tasted salty, sticky sweat that wet his shirt. His uncle looked out and down the street admiring what he hoped to never see again.

The next-door neighbor exited her house. "Hello, how is it going?"

"Fabulous, just like a garden of roses," he said as she walked across the street carrying a pot on top of her head filled with clothes. She mumbled under her breath.

"Yep, He's getting crazier and crazier. Just look at him." She smiled at him. They used to date. But everything had changed. He hadn't been with a woman in six months. But no one could tell from his gestures.

Tipi approached him with a sad pout. He took up the space between the door and his uncle. Nothing had changed, not even the scuba-tight pants. It drove him insane. People in the neighborhood began to call his uncle crazy behind his back.

"Tipi…" He paused for a second that felt like a lifetime. He held his face in his palms to hide his pain.

"Tipi…" He put his hands on his right shoulder. "…how would you like to come with me to work tonight? At least you won't be bored." He sighed, "You know Tipi, tonight is that night." He whispered. Kalargo's head lifted slowly. These were the best words he had ever heard. Before he replied, his uncle interrupted him. "We are leaving tonight. I've been waiting six months, six damn months!" A tear fell out of joy. "Tipi, say goodbye to Africa. You may never return."

His heartbeat began to race. He wanted to dream, scream and celebrate at the same time. He also remembered to keep calm.

Mugumbi planned to travel to the United States by ship as a stowaway. Only if the ship they had boarded was going to America. Due to his inability to read, they boarded a ship with an American flag that ended up in South Korea. After months of working under the table for slave wages, Mugumbi finally got a break. He met his future Korean American wife who introduced him to a prestigious individual, her stepfather, double agent Na Min Choi.

Kalargo's driver was steady talking, not realizing that his mind was far away until they pulled up to the gate of his house. He retrieved his PDA cell phone and used it to open the remote-controlled gate. She drove up to the driveway in the Hawaii Kai section of Honolulu.

"Home sweet home..." He dialed Na Min's number. He walked into his home with the cell phone to his ear. "Good afternoon. Mr. Choi, please."

He tossed his bags on the bed and pulled off his shirt and threw it in the basket of dirty clothes.

"Kalargo, are you feeling pretty good?"

He lay on the bed, tired. "I was wondering if we could meet later tonight and..."

Kalargo interrupted him "Well, hold on for a moment. I have to check my schedule", he came back. "Of course I have time."

He stood up, unclothed himself, and prepared his bathwater.

"I say after ten pm." The sound of bathwater can be heard in the background.

"You want to meet at Nicolis Nicolis?"

"Sure, why not. So then it is." They ended the conversation.

The huge bathroom covered with ivory pearl tile displayed a checkerboard design, ivory white sink, and brass faucets. The lit watermelon candles and bubble bath was exactly what he needed, relaxation. The Jacuzzi's pumps massaged his back while he closed his eyes under dim lights. He thought of how successful he wanted to be. He already owned one of the most popular martial arts and fitness spas on the island. But the bulk of his money came from international arms trade and distribution, sounds fancy. In reality, he supplied war-torn countries with weapons to fight. On his list was his native country The Gambia that needed his service.

The phone rang several times. "Who is bothering me now?" He opened his eyes and reached for the phone. "Yes, who's calling?"

His thick African accent could not be mistaken for anything other than a Gambian. He splashed water that can be heard in the background. He paused for a second or two.

"Hello." He said just before he pushed the button to end the call. He heard a female voice. It sounded like Jamie.

"I heard you playing with your rubber ducky." She said in a seductive voice that purred in his ear. He laughed and blew off her comment, in one ear and out the other.

"I thought you were my rubber ducky? Having fun?" With her lips, she made this sound that always excited him. He raised himself forward to pull the plug to the drain.

"Jamie, Could you call me back or I'll call you." He asked her. He hopped out of the deep Jacuzzi to dry off. She hesitated before she responded.

"You promise?"

"Well I tell you what; you call me in fifteen minutes. I should be dry by then." She agreed and they terminated the line.

The Hawaiian nights are what people enjoy, but the sun and beaches are what they come for. The weather attracted tourists from all parts of the globe. He rarely left the island. He was glad to be home. He lounged in his four-bedroom house surrounded by a seven-foot wall in one of the exclusive neighborhoods in Hawaii.

He entered the kitchen to prepare a snack. He wore his favorite white cotton robe, blue pajamas, and slippers that matched. His house was built to look and have an Oriental appeal. His admiration for the Korean was evident. He ate with chopsticks like they were born in his hand.

There was nothing he did not know. He cooked their food more and better than the Gambian. But he had a slightly different taste bud when it came to women. He had grown to be this debonair that he had dreamed of. He lived in Hawaii for ten years. He was lonely and missed his only family, Mugumbi.

He opened the fridge. "Well now..." He looked at the baked chicken, noodles, and a plate jeon. He grabbed a little of everything just to satisfy all his taste buds. He spoke out loud. "I guess a little red wine..." He tuned out loud. "...should not hurt the mind, at least not this time."

He grabbed a flute-shaped glass and walked into the living room under dim lights. He picked up the remote control. "Hmm..." With one touch, the wall unit rose from the floor and the entertainment center appeared. "Do I want to watch T.V., listen to jazz?" He hit the music button, "maybe some Jazz." He flopped into the colossal circular black sofa. "Spanish Jazz, I 'm in the mood for." He looked at his watch and noticed it was nearly eight-thirty. He picked up the phone to call Jamie. The ring tone buzzed his ear and his eyes watched the EQ on the stereo, jazz filtered the entire house.

"Hello, this is Jamie..." Kalargo sighed. "Hey what's up? You are kind of late calling." He was interrupted with a rueful voice. "Can you hold?" It caught him off guard and he had to wait a moment. She finally came back with this cheerful voice.

"I am so sorry, who is this?" Like a dummy, he spoke into the machine. "This is Kalargo."

"I am not in at the moment. Please leave a short to the point message. I'll get a hold of you verbally, mentally, physically, or joyfully. Thank you." He grinned.

"She gets me every time. Yeah, Jamie, I call to say hello and to return your call..." A buzzer interrupted him. He stood up to check his monitor. "Anyway just call me" He slid the phone into his robe pocket.

"Are you going to let me in?" Jamie stood at the gate camera. She hopped into her car.

"Of course, park your car next to the Lexus. Make sure to be careful, I just had the roses planted."

Jamie stood 5'7, long curly blonde hair with a pecan-like tan with crystal sky blue eyes. Jamie was born in San Diego and lived on the island ever since her parents separated. Upon meeting him, she worked at a fruit market for three years on the side of the road in an unpopulated section of the island.

After she parked her car, she double-checked to make certain there was space between the Lexus. "How's it?" She said and embraced him and pushed her tongue down his throat.

"Well, you know as usual."

"Come on in, I'm having a glass of wine. She made herself comfortable. She sat her black purse on the sofa and sighed as she had never been there before.

"So how was your flight?" She chose a champagne glass.

"You want champagne or wine?" He held a bottle of each in both hands.

"I'll have whatever you are having." She held her glass up and watched the wine pour. She looked at him with a cunning gesture and sipped a little before she took her glass to the sofa and sat down like a lady.

"My day was boring. I arrived on the afternoon flight; actually, it was delayed due to a layover in the Philippines. Other than that I was listening to some Jazz."

"So how is your dad?" She crossed her legs.

"Actually He's doing fine. I am meeting him tonight. What are you doing later? He would love to see you." He sat next to her. She watched T.V. with her glass touching her lips. "Nothing really, I wanted to spend some time with you."

He stood up and looked at his watch. "I guess you wouldn't mind coming with me to meet him?" He headed toward the master suite but could be heard. "Then we can go to the beach afterward."

"Should I change my clothes?" She sat the glass on the table, stood from the sofa, and entered the kitchen.

"You know I like to go to the beach, especially at night." He came from the master suite "Yati yati yati, we both know why you like the beach."

She was in front of the open fridge picking grapes from the bag. She tossed a couple of them in her mouth. Suddenly he came from behind with a loving embrace. He put his lips on the back of her neck. His body pressed against hers.

She wore a pair of skintight jeans that made her look luscious. She grinds her buttocks into his midsection.

"Now you know you like to tease and keep me hungry for you." She looked over her shoulder.

"Why would I…" The ringing of his cellular phone interrupted her.

"What time is it?" He asked looking down at his watch.

"Nine-fifteen." He sighed.

"Yes hello." He walked away from Jamie. The voice on the phone quickly put a smile on his voluptuous lips. He moved far enough to talk in private.

"So how is it going on your end?" The voice asked him.

"Very well, I sent the package. It should arrive in less than four hours. The commander is part of the flight crew. He should be contacting you one hour after they land to inform you where to meet him." he walked into an unoccupied part of the house and then entered his office.

"Everything is cool but what about the other crew members?" "As I said, everything is under control. Nobody else knows a thing. It's what they call, TOP SECRET. We are taking this seriously."

"Well, until then I'll wait on the call and I'll be near the base in a couple of hours. I'll talk to you later, out." They both ended the phone call.

Chapter Two

The blazing sun glared on the ocean that made a mirror reflection. It was amazing how beautiful and calm a huge body of water could be. The Indian Ocean can be lonely at times but once in a while, the calm and peaceful waters are disturbed by an U.S.S. aircraft carrier. The U.S.S. Carl Vinson operated a hundred miles off the island of Diego Garcia, population six hundred; the island was three miles wide and twenty-eight miles long. One of the beautiful islands that Great Britain owned and is not known to many. It was used as a military installation. The battle group cruised towards the North Arabian Sea. It carried a crew of five thousand and over fifty aircraft of various squadrons. Squadron VRC-50 was the most loved and expected aircraft to land. The twin-turboprop C-2 better known as the GREYHOUND delivered passengers, parts, and most important, mail. Its day or night, long-range capabilities and any weather were perfect for Naval Logistics. The squadron was stationed out of Cubi Point Naval Air station, Philippines. The squadron detached personnel aboard the carrier to assist in logistics. The sound of a C-2 was like Xmas every time.

"Good morning, how does the flight deck look?" The leading Petty Officer entered the small cramped workspace crowded with toolboxes and six sailors waiting to recover an aircraft.

"Well, the ETA says fourteen hundred hours but we got to have it ready for the next flight cycle.

A voice mumbled out. "Ok, it's thirteen thirty now. In about ten minutes. I want to be up on the flight deck and ready. I don't want the air boss breathing down my neck and chewing my ass out for not recovering our own bird. He took a seat on the edge of the desk.

"Airman Crockett, do a quick turnaround. It doesn't have to be too thorough, just look for the obvious and write it down. I know it's your first time out at sea. And you are the plane captain but out here we are one team, one family. We pitch in. Basically, we don't do major maintenance out here unless we absolutely have to. If you find something, let me know, write it down. We'll let the crew back on land handle it. Oh, by the way, make sure you put your order in for whatever you need from base." He sat there like a big shot with goggles on the top of his cranial like a tank commander.

"The other squadrons don't mind helping us out with supplies only because we do them favors. So stock supplies for the minor problems."

His dingy olive-green fatigues were tucked in his unpolished boots. A crew of six included an aviation mechanic, structural/hydraulic, electrician, avionics, plane captain, and a Q/A quality and assurance, just enough to get the job done.

"Did they say what they were carrying?" Airman Crockett asked while sitting on top of a toolbox holding a pair of gloves in his hand. He looked like he was expecting his Japanese girlfriend to jump out of a birthday cake.

"Well I'm not sure but I do know they have about ten passengers and two weeks of backed-up mail." The leading Petty Officer said.

Airman Crockett stood 5'9, twenty years old with a military haircut, a hundred seventy pounds, an African American from Miami Florida. He just arrived at the squadron eight months ago.

"Well, it's about that time." The leading Petty Officer headed out the iron integrity door of the ship. The workspace was located just below the flight deck, starboard aft section. There is a sixty-foot drop into the ocean if anyone wants to free dive. Not like it has not been done before by lonely sailors who are in desperate need to go home. The catwalk was made of iron and it led to the flight deck. You could hear and see the waves that splashed against the side of the ship through the iron that was beneath your feet.

The catapult can be felt as it launches the fighter jets and bombers. Even with ear protection, you can barely hear the person next to you screaming in your ear. The use of hand signals told everyone when what, and where to go on the flight deck. The fumes that hovered the mini airport from more than fifteen planes at any given time are just as dangerous. The exhaust from any one of them could blow you off the flight deck into the ocean, worst-case scenario, to be blown into the engine of another plane.

Petty Officer, E-7, the quality assurance officer and leader of the detachment, the career type was born in Paris, Texas, a country fellow that spoke with a deep drawl. He is a dishwater blonde redhead that stood 5'11, two hundred thirty pounds. The Petty Officer walked over to Airman Crockett.

"Now look, the air boss wants the C-2 parked next to the island of the aircraft carrier, just below the flight control center. You won't be shutting the engines down. They will unload and take off. Ok?" He screamed in the direction of his earmuff. He spoke over the loud engines that were at high power six feet away.

"There she is." The C-2 was pointed out circling the ship in between the high clouds; it looked like a flying dot. It did donuts around the carrier waiting for its chance to land. There is no other aircraft that looked as dangerous as the wide fat big nose short C-2 landing on the flight deck. You have to imagine the ship shifting left to right and up and down according to the motion of the ocean. Then the C-2 Greyhound trying to land, believe me, it is a sight to see. And do not forget about the wind that drifts the plane as it tries to land.

As the plane approached for landing, the flight deck firemen and other crew members were on standby. Not more than one mile out, it took the last fly by before it descended. The C-2 lined up with lighting that guided the plane in. A long trail of exhaust smoke lingered behind the turboprop as it struggled to line itself for landing. It looked like it would crash into the ocean or the ship.

"On deck! On deck!" The flight deck loudspeaker said. The plane quickly full-throttled in case they missed four of the landing cables they have in place to catch them. The tail hook lifted, and they taxied to the island. Not more than two minutes later an F-14 landed and the process continued.

After unloading passengers and mail the leading Petty Officer sent a crew member to the workspace with two unbelievable flat boxes two and a half by fifteen inches. "What! Pizza Hut! Hot damn, Pizza Hut in the middle of the ocean! Where did that come from?" Airman Crockett yelled.

"It came from where we are going next..." Petty Officer Ramsey yelled back, "...North Arabian Sea?" The guy smiled and walked off, "War baby."

The C-2 was directed to the catapult and ready for takeoff. Like a slingshot, it was thrown off the front of the ship at a minimum of one hundred fifty miles per hour.

Moments later, the phone rang in the VRC-50 workspace. They had slices of pizza in their mouths and gobbling like wild turkeys.

"VRC-50 this is a nonsecure line how can I help you sir or maim?" P.O. Ramsey had licked his lips and fingers while holding the phone with his shoulder.

"This is the air boss, did they deliver the pizza?"

"Yes sir, it should be there. It's already in route."

"Tell your crew, job well done..." he added a couple of more words and ended the call.

Several hours had passed and the sun was swallowed by the horizon that made a cloudless night filled with stars. At any given time you could make a wish to a fallen star. Airman Crockett looked out into the pitch darkness knowing that only the battle group was near. Flight operations went on until 2200 hours.

"Well, it's about that time to hit the rack." He looked at his watch and sighed. "We don't have to be up until what, 1330 hours?" He looked at the POD plan of the day to verify when the next C-2 will arrive.

The voice of the Captain of the ship bellowed the speaker of the 1-M-C that the entire ship can hear. "This is the Captain, I would like to have everyone's attention for a moment. Today was a fine working day. Currently, I would like to give an AT a Boy to squadron VF-120 and VA-140 for doing an excellent job on their bomb runs. It was carried out expeditiously without injuries. However we all know that we all work as a team, a ship is nothing without its crew. I also know that it is a little hard on some of us being away from family and loved ones for such a long period of time. In three days it'll be Christmas and..." The captain paused. "Yes, it's a difficult time. But we are out here making sure the international sea lanes are open and not controlled by countries who wish to do harm or take over countries that can't take up for themselves. So yes, as the most powerful country in the world, we have a job to do, an obligation to protect international waters." He cleared his throat and continued.

"I just got word today that our mission has changed. The chief of Naval Operations has given us the orders to be on standby due to Saddam Hussein's

Army attacking Kuwait. At this very moment, we are full speed ahead to the Persian Gulf in what is now called the Arabian Sea."As the Captain spoke, Airman Crockett could feel the mood change among his crew. It humbles some; it got serious all of a sudden. He wondered, will this be war? He had noticed weeks earlier that they had replenished the carrier with bombs and the practice flights had increased dramatically. He also remembered that another group of his squadron was detached to Manama, Bahrain, fifty miles from Saudi Arabia and three hundred miles from Kuwait. He knew that was within scud missile range. He thought about the threat of gas attacks and chemical suits. He shook his head and sighed. The buildup of more battle groups were being positioned and there were two battle groups already there, U.S.S. Midway, U.S.S. Enterprise. He thought about what the President of the United States said, "War is imminent."

* * *

Two weeks later, under an unforgiving blistering sun that made sweat feel like boiling water on the flight deck with high powered exhaust hot enough to melt your skin beneath a brown turtleneck sweater. Airman Crockett carried a set of three chains to secure the C-2 to the flight deck to prevent the plane from shifting when the ship rocks and rolls. The leading Petty Officer walked over to him.

"Hey, after you secure the C-2 we have a meeting, so don't disappear.

"What's the meeting about?"

"We have to go over our tools and get ready to take off. We are flying to Bahrain first thing in the morning. The bird is spending the night. So after we go over some details as a group, be ready for a catapult take off."

"Damn, flying off the ship." he sighed.

Later that night he barely slept because he could not stop thinking about this catapult take off. He had seen it many times and now, he has to experience it. He felt like the C-2 Greyhound now looked like a flying coffin instead of looking like a friendly snoopy. He slept in a coffin rack that was the size of a real coffin, maybe seven feet long by three feet wide. The berthing quarters stacked the coffin-like beds three up and three in front of him, a very small space where he had to lift his bed to put all of his belongings. If it doesn't fit, you don't need it.

The 0430 wake-up call was a tapping noise on the edge of the rack. "It is that time." A fellow crew member gave him a wake-up call.

Do I have time to cat?" He asked with a war-ending breath that he covered with the sheet.

"We have box lunches ready for us on the plane. The in-flight plane captain has already picked those up, by the way, have you ever taken off from an aircraft carrier?"

"No." He peeked through the sheets that had covered his head.

"Well, there is a first time for everything." He walked away with a grin.

The C-2 had to be the slowest aircraft the Navy had. The flight was like riding a snail with wings. It would take a fighter thirty minutes to fly from where the ship was located. The C-2 took two hours and thirty minutes to arrive in Bahrain. Airman Crockett closed his eyes and thought about the very first time he landed in a foreign country.

Eight months ago

The night was hot, humid, and beautiful at the same time. He knew he was in a whole new world. The people were different by culture, language, habit, and much more. The Philippine women, you could not ask for any more exotic. The short, dark skin almond eyes with jet-black hair and their accent, was mind-blowing. He was dropped into heaven without a white flag.

"Have you heard about the game called QUARTERS?" A passenger asked him.

"This guy knows where all the good spots to go to, you coming?"

He frowned, "Naa, You guys go without me. I already know about QUARTERS."

His dream was interrupted when the in-flight plane captain shook his shoulder.

"We are landing in five minutes." He went around waking up everyone who was sleeping.

He sighed and opened his eyes. He looked out the window and

saw dessert for miles. "Wow! Now, this is a whole new world."

* * *

Honolulu, Hawaii

Jamie slept through the night having the same horrific dream. She mumbled words that Kalargo ignored until she almost gagged. In her dream, she was jogging on a trail like she usually does.

"I'm going jogging along the trail. I'll be back within the hour." She spoke into her answering machine. She exited the house wearing her red tights and white t-shirt with a pouch around her waist. She went back into the house to change her batteries for her walkman headset. She also grabbed her best cassette tape, Phil Collins.

"Where are you?" she called and whistled for her cute annoying black chiwawa with a little bit of brown on its belly. Ziggy ran from the pet entrance of the door that swung in both directions.

"Come on Ziggy. It's time for our morning run. He wagged his tail and moved around like he had been waiting on her the whole time. He jumped into the grass from the porch and took his ritual pump and morning dump. After he finished he turned around to smell it, licked it, and backed away from it.

It was a perfect morning to jog under a cloudless sky with pockets of fog that looked like they floated just above the ground along the green grassy trail. Some people referred to Jamie as a health addict and others just labeled her as drop-dead gorgeous.

After a mile and a half, her heartbeat was at a normal jogger's beat on a trail that she jogged at least three times a week. She arrived at her turn-around point and noticed that Ziggy was not behind her. She stopped and removed her headphones. She began to trace backward.

"Ziggy!" She yelled out his name. She listened. Suddenly Ziggy came from the bushes.

"There you are!" She was relieved. But Ziggy stood there and looked into the bushes. He wagged his tail and barked two times. The closer she got, the further he would go into the bushes. She sighed.

"I don't have time for this. Come on boy." She begged him.

Ziggy peaked out of a small hole between the bushes like he was calling her, as soon as she got closer. He took off behind the bushes again. It was like a game he played.

When she walked through the bushes and pulled huge leaves aside to make her way. She saw a black man hanging upside down from a tree. His blood dripped like a faucet, and his face was swollen like water balloons. She grabbed her chest with her right hand and covered her mouth with her left. It was as if the two guys that beat him mercifully could not see her standing there. The body moved on every strike until they stopped beating him. She walked closer with tears in her eyes, "Stop! What are you doing?" She asked them.

They ignored her like she was invisible. The closer she got, the more she realized that she was like a ghost. She dropped to her knees and pleaded with the two soldiers to stop beating him.

"You are going to kill him!" She screamed from the bottom of her lungs and pulled on her shirt like she was going to rip it off. "What are you doing?!" She reached for his hand.

His eyes opened as blood spilled from his mouth like a gutted pig. She crawled over to him and grabbed his bloody hand that barely touched the dirt that had mixed together. She squeezed his hand tight.

"Wake up Jamie! Hey, you must be having a bad dream." He held her hand.

Her eyes opened wide and she jumped away from him like he was the attacker.

"Are you going to be ok?" He sighed and got her a glass of water.

She looked around with sweat on her forehead. She scratched her chest and rubbed her nose. Her bloodshot wet eyes made her realize that she was safe, but her scratches on her chest and the tears from the corner of her eyes said otherwise.

"My God," She swallowed a dry throat of saliva, "was I talking in my sleep?" She asked him.

"What! You were mumbling and moaning something, looked like you were having a..." He was interrupted. "...A nightmare on Elm Street." He laughed and gave her some water.

"What were you dreaming about?"

"I..." She sighed. "I can't remember." She paused and cuddled with him.

"I can't believe I do not know what I was dreaming about. I'm pretty sure it will come to me sooner or later." She lay there with his favorite white robe on with nothing else beneath. Her beautiful lips and facial features gave her a VIP pass to anywhere.

"Hold me." He kissed her on the neck and embraced her.

"Are you hungry? I cooked breakfast while you were sleeping."

She inhaled and smelt fresh eggs and bacon.

"Yes, love to eat" She stood up and tightened the robe around

her. His beeper went off. He looked down and picked up the phone.

"I tell you what..." She walked into the kitchen. "...I'll fix my plate, you answer your beeper." She grabbed two plates for them both.

Chapter Three

"Na Min, what's going on? I am surprised to hear from you this early."

"Good morning to you too, I think we have a problem. The shipment we got several weeks ago."

Kalargo is outside opening his car door. "What about it?"

He heard him sigh, "All of that has to be shipped out. There is another shipment coming in tomorrow. From what I understand, it needs to go ASAP." He became quiet.

He was caught by surprise. He pondered while he sat in his car. "Does it have to be done tonight?" He sounded like a kid on punishment. "My contact is not able to move anything right now. I have no way to get trucks." He rubbed his left pinky finger on his left collarbone below where his scar was.

"The ship will be docked in the harbor. The name is "RUSH" Captain Tomzach will be expecting your arrival three hours before their departure. If you have to rent the trucks, do it. We have people counting on this."

Kalargo spoke and thought at the same time, "Tell them Handyman is on the move." They ended the call. He looked in the rearview mirror to pick a fight with a painful nose hair. Then he quickly dialed a number from memory.

"Bennett, yeah good morning, wake up. Hey, I know you can hear me."

A voice responded. "What are you doing calling me so early?" He coughed and spat into the trash.

"We got work to do tonight." He explained.

"What time is it?" He laid his head on the pillow.

"It's Ten am but by ten tonight, we need to have everything loaded on the dock."

Bennett stopped him, "Tonight! I thought…"

"I know what you thought, I said the same thing. Grab ten of your guys, don't worry they will be paid well as usual. Because of the short notice, I will rent the trucks."

He sighed with his head under the pillow with the phone to his mouth. "I guess I could be ready in a couple of hours." He tried to hang up the phone but Kalargo got a couple of last words in. "I'll call you at six o'clock on the dot. Have them ready." The line went dead.

Jamie tiptoed towards the car like she was modeling on top of hot stones for a pageant with no shoes on. "Your breakfast is getting cold. Did you want milk or orange juice?"   She leaned forward with her hands on her knees still in his robe. "Orange juice." They both walked hand in hand into the house.

* * *

"Yes, I would like to speak to Zang please."

Na Min stood 5'6 with a receding hairline and gray streaks that blended among his straight hair that touched his shoulder. He was an expert in computer programming and the gathering of Tactical Intelligence. He spoke four languages and held a black belt in martial arts. He trained Kalargo in his younger days. Because he was a Korean American and spoke Korean it gave him the ability to be a good spook until he turned. He was born in Korea raised in Seattle. At the age of thirty, he became a leading Agent and a Double Agent for the North Koreans. He had moved so far up the ladder. He had frequent meetings with the President of the United States to personally inform him of the North Koreans nuclear technology advancement, troop movement, and activities. But what Agent Na Min did not inform him on was their activities outside the borders of the North Korean peninsula.

"Yes Na Min, How is it going in Hawaii?" Zang spoke in Korean.

"I am calling to inform you that the equipment should be on the move tonight. Now you said the next load should be in tomorrow. But nothing changes, right?" he waited for his response.

"That will be right. I know this is premature; however, I am sorry for the short notice. Everything's going well..." Agent Na Min was interrupted.

"How's the weather?" Zang asked. They both grinned.

* * *

Kalargo's house

The whole house smelt like fried eggs, bacon, and sausages that floated past their noses.

"Tell me when too much." She put eggs on the plate until he held his hand up to signal that's enough. He tossed a couple of strips of bacon, and sausages on the plate and parked his rear end on the sofa. They watched T.V. and enjoyed each other's company.

"Is there any more apple juice?" He spoke with a piece of bacon between his teeth and talked at the same time.

"Actually I had the last glass of apple juice last night. The only thing left is orange juice, grapefruit, and milk." She looked in the fridge with half of the sausage in her right hand and the other half in her mouth. "Mix orange juice and fruit punch." he requested. She frowned like that was a nasty combination. "I never mix my drinks." She carefully gave it to him and sat next to him. She leaned over and sucked his lips with a wet kiss. "I love you." She said.

"I love you too," Kalargo responded.

"What are you watching?" she reached for the remote.

"Nothing really, you can change it if you want," he told her with his plate on his lap just behind his knees.

In the past couple of months, their relationship had grown to more serious than a physical attraction. They bonded so well until they knew mentally that they were meant for each other. But at times she felt like he was too busy for her with work, travel, and the fitness spa. He never thought he was ready to settle down for something as serious as this. He never pressured her into bed and gave her the utmost respect. At one point she thought he was gay because he had held out for so long. She was convinced, all that had changed when she was allowed to spend the night. For all the time she had waited was so worth that one night of a Jacuzzi bath filled with French vanilla milk and rose petals floating all around them. The lit candles dripped and filled the bathroom with a cotton candy smell. He picked her up in his arms and let the milk drip dry with rose petals sticking to her wet body. She knew she would never receive treatment like this from anyone remotely close. He had her when he first poured warm milk on the back of her neck, chest, and hair. The red and white colors were mind-blowing; she knew that he knew how to treat a woman to the fullest.

He took his plate into the kitchen "You know what today's date is?"

"I think it's the twenty-second of Dec." She responded.

"Do you have to work tomorrow?" he asked.

"Why?" she asked.

"I just wanted to know if you wanted to work out anytime soon." The faucet water can be heard as he put his plate in the sink. "Matter of fact, I need to start getting ready, order the rental trucks, oh yeah let me double-check on Bennett." He walked into the bedroom to change clothes. "Knowing him he went back to sleep..." He thought about it and put the phone down, "...actually, he's pretty reliable." He mumbled to himself. Due to short notice, he was only able to rent six trucks and they had to be picked up by seven pm.

"Jamie, I might have to leave early. What are your plans?"

She walked out of the bathroom flossing her teeth and talking at the same time.

"I should be ready..." She pulled the floss through her back molars "...as soon as I wash up."

He walked across a gray Persian rug as he entered his office and tapped on the keyboard of his computer to secure the perimeter of his home at three pm. He stood up and retrieved a hand full of fish food from the shelf behind him to feed his piranhas that looked hungry.

His office looked like a corporate space but the size of a bedroom. The thick glass table that held his computer was neatly organized. The blue light in the fish tank exposed the coral reef that he handpicked from Central America. The two marble chiseled tribesmen stood 5 feet with spears and a shield in their hands with twenty-four karat gold eyes. He walked over to his safe and dabbled with the keypad. It beeped and opened on its own.

"OK, three clips." He grabbed his custom made Chinese Mauser chrome .45 caliber nickel plated, pearl handle with gold screws and aim sight that he got from his dad as a gift. It was engraved, "Life or Death, You choose." It was last produced in the 1920s or 1930s, the Chinese markings on the side meant "Type One". He shoved it in his shoulder holster and slid his arms through. Before he walked out he activated the security alarm.

"Are you ready?" He yelled as he threw on his windbreaker to hide his armor. When he looked into the room she was sliding into her pink thongs with purple butterfly prints. He went to the car. She came out and kissed him on the cheek.

"Hey call me later." They closed their doors and drove off.

The overcast had passed making the sky partly cloudy with a slight wind from the east of the beautiful glittering ocean. He could see cargo ships out on the horizon and he knew one of them was a cargo ship named "RUSH". He looked at his car clock and noticed that traffic wasn't heavy as usual. For it to be two forty-five, that was good he thought, less time he'll have to deal with stupid drivers. His thoughts were interrupted by his cellular.

"Bennett, I knew I could count on you."

"Don't do your counting yet, I was only able to get four men." he can hear Kalargo spitting up cuss words in Korean that he couldn't understand.

"Where is everyone?" he vehemently asked

"Two guys are on the big island and..."

Kalargo's vehemence would have blown a radiator cap, "Bennett! " He paused to calm down. He let out a sigh from deep down. "Beeeenneeet, listen. Do whatever you need to do to bring the original crew together. Or else tonight will be a long night." He paused to make a right turn to get on the Queen Liliuokalani freeway. "Have four of the guys meet at your place at five o'clock. I'm on my way, should be there in forty-five minutes. That way we could have the trucks in position." They both agreed and ended the phone call.

Chapter Four

Waikiki beach was crowded with tourists trying to get the ultimate super tan. On a partly cloudy day with showers that had just passed would not stop them from waiting on the beach for the sun to come out. Kalargo drove down Kalakaua Ave and pulled into Kuhio Beach Park parking meter on the beachfront. He sat there just watching the kids play in the sand, and diving off the concrete wall into the waves that rushed the shoreline. He noticed the different cultures that walked and tanned on the beach. A gay couple passed his car holding hands. The volleyball was being chased and kept above ground. Through all of this was like watching a silent scream movie from the interior of his car. He realized that he pulled into the parking lot to get a burger from Jack in the Box. Suddenly he opened his door and beach life was in full swing.

He returned to his car from Kapahulu Ave with a combo meal. He noticed how dirty his car was. He opened the car door and sat his food on the passenger seat. It was this moment he thought about a friend of his that was killed fifteen years ago in Seoul, South Korea.

On a cold night with snow flurries falling like ash from a distant fire. He was on his way to meet Yhong, a nice fellow, bright and handsome dark tanned Korean. He was supposed to deliver documents that were classified. He found him shot in the head and one bullet in the chest. Did he betray Na Min? Did the Chinese kill him? All these unanswered questions routinely tiptoed back into his mind. It was something Yhong wanted to tell him. But by the time he reached him his lungs were drowning him in his own blood. There was nothing he could do but run and avoid questioning. If he had not been late. He could have helped him or got a bullet.

By the time he reached Mugumbi's house, he was nervous and paced around trying to explain. "Yhong is dead!" he sat down with his palms shielding his face.

He could remember how limp his body was, he was trying to tell him something before he pulled and tugged with his bloody hands on his gray and white button-down shirt. He died with Kalargo's ear to his lips.

Mugumbi had just walked into the house thirty minutes before he did. He was not surprised by this news. Did he know about this already? Kalargo did not know what kind of work he was doing for Na Min so he would have not suspected his own uncle to be the killer.

Mugumbi's first executive party put ten thousand U.S. dollars in his hands. It was his secret between him and Na Min. He was a tall Gambian with a three-inch Afro, faded on the side, with deep sunken eyes that looked like he was on a hunger strike. His lips were a distinctive and very much African that was under a neatly trimmed thick mustache. He always maintained a successful appearance that hid his addiction to heroin.

The drug relaxed him as he listened to Kalargo and thought about his first executive party. The mood, weather, atmosphere, location, and the

38

fact that he had never forgotten, he was so nervous and scared. The key to the judge's house and the security code was in Mugumbi's possession. The family was on vacation and he stood in all black in his closet of the master bedroom suite. He remembered the small bubbles of sweat that slowly rolled one by one down the curved valley that followed the spine of his back. The masked that revealed the bloodshot red eyes that gave death no chance to run or hide. The heavy steel revolver that was heavier with a silencer. His hands shook and the feeling of moving earthworms crawled on the bottom of his stomach.

The sound of the brakes came to a halt when the judge pulled in front of his house. He took a deep breath, gripped his revolver and tightened the silencer. He held the weapon three inches in front of his face. He held a picture of the judge in his left hand and waited. Suddenly, Mugumbi had realized his day-dream was over and was back in the kitchen, listening to Kalargo babble on about Yhong.

"I can't believe someone would want to kill him," Mugumbi said to comfort him.

Mugumbi's drug addiction started two months after the death of the judge. His now-wife Yuki a beautiful exotic Asian lured him in with love and a habit that paid a price. The drug helped him cope with his feelings. The two things he had never forgotten, his first kill and the first hit of heroin. He can remember the first time he used it as if it was yesterday. She came in from getting her daily dosage of heroin. The sound of church bells can be heard on this Sunday afternoon under a blue sky with warm intentions. He had wished like hell he could shoot whoever was pulling the damn rope to that bell. The traffic of churchgoers passed slowly.

Yuki was no more than 5'5, a hundred fifteen pounds, and pale complexion with the most gorgeous eyes. She desired a bigger rack on her chest, but her buttocks compensated her for that. Her denim jeans, two-inch heels, and a blue leather double-breasted coat that was knotted with her belt. Her new haircut gave her a younger look.

"Hey baby..." he said as she walked in the room. She put her purse on the bed. "How are you feeling?" she asked him. She kicked off her heels and pushed them under the foot of the bed.

"Did you come back with..." she interrupted him. "Are you sure you want to try this?" she held the small baggy in between her right thumb and index fingers. He put his hands on top of hers.

"Yuki..." he paused. "If... it helps me to forget my past and my pain. If it numbs me and makes me feel good like you say it does..." he nodded his head. "I gotta have it."

He never told her the real reason, just some made up a tale about The Gambian police beatings, hangings of his family and friends that haunted him. She also would have never guessed that he was a hitman. He was good at keeping her out of his business.

"Now my love..." she spoke with a syringe horizontally between her lips. She wrapped the belt around his right arm just above his elbow and tightened it to expose his veins. She was teary-eyed as a falling tear landed on the crease of his inner elbow; it was like hot acid that boiled into his dark black skin. It slowly made its way down and crossed his uprooted like veins. She sighed as she pulled the cap off the syringe and squirted a little. She used her forearm to wipe her runny eyes to clear her vision for a better aim. She wanted to explain what he should expect but she was interrupted.

"Please, just do it." He begged to get it over with as the needle pinched his skin. His blood mixed with the heroin in the syringe. When she pulled the handle to make sure she had a vein. Then she slowly and carefully pushed the handle of the syringe to insert the brownish liquid monster that will love, neglect, disappoint, numb, and embrace him like no other. His marriage and love affair will be a rocky boundless one that will only give him a temporary escape and a dream that will only make him more vulnerable. Mugumbi realized that he had drifted into a daydream and Kalargo was standing over the kitchen sink trying to clean his shirt of Yhong's blood. "Uncle, what do you think is going on?"

40

* * *

Waikiki Beach

Back at the beach

The sound of kids passed Kalargo's car as he chewed on a cold French fry with his half-empty cup. All this was going through his mind while sitting at the beach. He tossed a French fry in his mouth and took a good chunky bite of his burger. He wondered what his uncle was up to these days. He picked up his cellular phone and licked his fingers of ketchup and dialed a number.

"Hello Bennett, are you ready? Do you have everything?" he asked. He replied with an assuring voice.

"Of course, we are waiting for you," Bennett said.

He cranks his car. "OK, I'm on my way." And ended the call, he opened his door and tossed the remaining food towards the trash can and missed. He rushed to meet Bennett.

He entered Bennett's house and was immediately approached by him, "Listen, I was only able to round up six trucks. It may take a while but we'll get it done on time."

Moments later they were on their way to the warehouse. Kalargo opened the last rusty metal door. "Yes…" he walked over to a stockpile of wooden crates. He repositioned his holster inside his jacket. He stood over a crate that he was about to open. The sound of forklifts and motors revved up, and the loading had begun.

"OK, let me see what I'm sending to my homeland?" he pulled out an RPG-7. The crate contained ten of them. The forklifts continued to load the other crates. In total the shipment manifested Mauser C96's, assault rifles(AK's), light machine guns RPK's and RPD's), M-37's,M-38's, anti-armor(RPG-16's), B-10's, M-42's, F-1 anti-personnel hand grenades, DS-39's, SG-43 Godunov's, AVS-36's, M1911A1's, Russian M1938's, PPSH41's, DP Ruchnoy Pulemyot light machine guns, RG-42 grenades, and Nambu pistols type 14.

He rolled up his manifest list and tucked it in his back pocket and jumped on a forklift to help load the crates. His cellular rung as he maneuvered the forklift, "Hello."

"Hey what's going on?" the voice sounded familiar. He looked at the screen and realized that it was a Philippine country code. It had to be Jenko.

"Hey, where were you? I was just in the Philippines, I tried to get a hold of you." He was excited to hear from his childhood friend.

"I changed my number not long ago. I've been so busy with my new business, man it's crazy. But I finally settled in and this is my new number." Jenko said.

"Jenko…"

"Yeah?" Jenko said.

"I am so in the middle of something." He put the phone down and yelled at his workers, "Come on people, let's stay on schedule!" He returned to his conversation. "Are you going to be up later?" Kalargo asked.

"Hey finish what you're doing and give me a call. Any time, Oh before I forget, you think you'll be able to come here for the martial arts competition in July?"

"Wow, now that is a good question…" he stopped the forklift to wait to load the next load. He leaned on the wheel, "…I can't really say. I have not missed one yet, but if I can't I will give you a call. Hey, keep in touch and stop being a stranger." The line was dead after they said their goodbyes. The two of them had been friends since teenagers. They competed against each other in martial arts and Jenko felt second to him to this very day.

"Hey Bennett, how many crates are left to be loaded?" He climbed down from the forklift and pulled himself up on the truck to tie down the cargo.

"Thirty more, we should be done in fifteen minutes."

"OK listen, meet me at the dock. I'll take three drivers with me so I can start unloading on the ship. The RUSH is at pier 89." He looked at his watch. "I need three of you to drive!" he yelled over Bennett's shoulder. "I'll see you there in no more than thirty minutes." He quickly walked away and returned to his supervisory mode.

He pulled out his cellular and noticed that he had four missed calls from Jamie. He decided not to call.

Then he noticed a missed call from Na Min.

"Good morning…" he always spoke to him in Korean to keep him in practice. "How is it going, on schedule?"

"Of course, the first three loads are on the way. I'm in the first truck."

"I'll call Tomzach." They both ended the line.

* * *

The shipping docks were quiet with an occasional ship horn that echoed through the harbor of darkness. The thick fog draped the bay like wet curtains that allowed the low flying screaming seagulls that flew over the choppy water searching for floating trash. The smell of matured exposed fruit with a mixture of caged animals lingered.

Among the ships are two cruise ships that frequently traveled from Waikiki to Los Angeles and three supercargo ships down there was a small beat up two hundred yard rust can known as the "RUSH". Captain Tomzach peered through his binoculars. He stood in a crimson trench coat with a white lapel and gold metallic buttons with two huge anchors on both sides. He was 5'11, 230 lbs Russian that spoke fluent Korean and horrible English. He looked like a fifty-year-old who just graduated from boot camp. His Russian accent rolled off his tongue. "Get that crane ready and put this load aft of the ship on the starboard."

"Yes, they are on time." He said and looked down at his wristwatch. He picked up the ship's phone to inform his crew to prepare for loading.

Kalargo stepped out of the truck before it came to a complete stop. He directed the following trucks to wait in line. He waved to Captain Tomzach and approached the ramp of the ship.

"Welcome aboard." The captain greeted him with a firm handshake. "Is everything going accordingly?"

Kalargo sighed, "As planned, are they ready to load them?"

The captain held up his left index finger, "My men are always ready." He looked him in the eyes. He picked up the ship's phone and gave a command in horrible English to start loading.

After two hours, the eastern morning sky commenced to brighten and the herd of shipyard employees slowly dragged their feet like they were forced to go to a funeral. Kalargo's crew had finished just in time before shift changed and he stopped by the security gate to drop off a brown paper bag to the guard. They shook hands as the last truck passed. "Now you don't spend all that in one place."

"Oh don't worry Mr. Choi, I have a special place for it." He smiled and tucked it away behind his security belt until he got home.

Chapter Five

TheGambia, West Africa

The Gambia is located on the northwest coast of Africa and bordered Senegal. For many years it was not known for having any significant natural resources. Seventy percent depends on crops and livestock for its livelihood. A small-scale manufacturing activity features the process of peanuts, fish, and hide.

In a small village of Farafenni, Gambia, a Korean team of prospectors discovered the north of The Gambia river had an abundance of diamonds, gold, and oil. The civil war that lasted for more than twenty-five years had prevented the successes and growth. The North Koreans were supplying the rebels with weapons to overthrow King Shabonee with the help of double agent Na Min.

King Shabonee had two wives, three daughters, and two sons that died in a genocide blood bath. The village that spoke his native tongue had been burned to the ground, and to make sure that no one could claim the throne. Everyone in the village was beheaded. The rebels gutted pregnant women like fish to make sure there were no surviving sons.

But the King had one brother that did survive and gave him the position of General of the Gambian army. It would be thirty years later when he would find out that he had one son who escaped the genocide.

The civil war had replaced this beautiful country of green mountains, waterfalls, and culture friendly into a divided population. Attaining control of this government would bring prosperity to those living outside of this country. It's a new frontier that has not been touched. The most fascinating question is who would control these natural resources?

The United Nations has hesitated; neighboring countries have no desire to get involved. The country of Senegal closed its borders to over two hundred fifty-thousand refugees that now live along their border. These innocent people are dying by the hundreds. The King ordered all men, women, boys, and girls as young as twelve to bear arms. He would not allow the Gambian Islamic republic Army which is being funded with weapons by a communist country to overthrow his government.

King Shabonee sat in front of his bedroom window overlooking the city of Gunjur. His beautiful view of the North Atlantic Ocean was breathtaking. He held his oxygen mask to his face and fogged it with his breath. He had grown old, ill, but most importantly, still alive. A servant knocked on his door.

"Your majesty…" Paul slowly twisted the knob and peeked in. "…I hope I am not disturbing you, do you mind?"

The King looked over his shoulder and twisted himself to see him. "Paul?"

"Yes, it is me."

The King turned to his view watching the small fishermen coming in from the Ocean. He put his oxygen mask on his lap. "Come on in Paul, how is your day?"

Paul entered humbled with his hands along his side. "I have good news to report, the   General has taken control of the northern side of the river. The war is turning in our favor. He is doing an excellent job." He offered the King a cup of tea, "Morning tea?" He held the empty cup up before he poured the tea.

The King sighed as a relief that he has finally gained control of half of his country. He smiled and rubbed his chin. "Paul…" The King slowly stood and dragged his green oxygen tank to where he stood.

"Do you need…" before he could ask if he needed help walking. The King had refused.

"I think I will pour my own cup of tea today." he smiled at him and patted him on the shoulder. They celebrated with tea.

* * *

Honolulu, Hi

The sun slowly made its way through Kalargo's room. His right eye
slowly opened with eye snot in the corners, lucky his uncle was not
around. "Oh my god," He looked at the clock "damn, three o'clock
already." He batted his eyes to adjust his vision. He quickly covered his
face in the pillow and grunted. He felt hungry. But stood up, walked and
stretched his way towards the bathroom. The phone rang.

"Oh great timing, whoever it is can wait." He mumbled.

A message was not left. "I guess it wasn't that important."A few
moments later,

it rang again. He leaned over the toilet and urinated. He sighed. After the
third, he answered. "Hello."

There was silence for a moment, "Good afternoon." Her voice was
erotic as always. "I was trying to get a hold of you last night." She said.
Before he could respond, "How would you like to meet a friend of mine?
She's coming in from San Diego." She waited for his response.

He paused, "Well…" He tried to quickly think of what he had to do
later on that day, "hmmm, well I don't have anything planned, yeah why
not." His face was two inches away from the bathroom mirror softly
touching a zit. He frowned.

"I've told her about you…" she was interrupted.

"What time does her flight arrive?"

"She is going to call me when she arrives at her hotel. That should be around four o'clock. I'll call you, how does that sound?"

He sighed with a yawn that followed. "Good, I am just waking up. Make sure you call first." They ended the call.

After a quick shower, he splashed his favorite cologne on his abdomen and neck. He noticed the time and wondered how long he could live like this. He picked up his cell phone and dialed a long distance number. He waited patiently for an answer. Finally, he terminated the call. He walked into the kitchen but thought about where his uncle Mugumbi could be. For years he thought his uncle lived a modest life with his girlfriend.

He opened the refrigerator and grabbed a bowl of green seedless grapes, walked over to the French doors that overlooked the pool. He thought about his first murder. Though it was in self-defense, his true colors came out. He found out that his uncle was a hit man for the North Koreans. His thought took him back ten years, it was Perth, Australia. "Do you know these people?!"

"Make a left off the highway exit!" Mugumbi said before he could inquire for more information. His eyes were filled with fear, his forehead and armpits were sweaty. Before he could ask another question, there were more directions to follow.

It was three o'clock in the morning with patches of fog that crept slowly across the highway from a soiled field alongside. The nearest town outside of Perth was miles away. He drove at speeds up to a hundred twenty miles per hour. Their hearts were pumping like generators. The sweat that soaked their backs was uncomfortable and the last thing they wanted to think about. The rental car fishtailed as they ran a yellow light changed to red. Mugumbi looked back to see if they were still in the chase.

"What is the hell going on?!" he desperately wanted to know. Mugumbi opened the glove compartment and pulled out two desert eagles chrome pistols. He shoved the clips into them both.

"Damn..." He swallowed and sighed, "What did I get myself into?" he mumbled.

Mugumbi could not, by all means, tell him about the assassinations of this list of wealthy and powerful people. They both frequently looked into the mirrors. But Mugumbi sighed and decided not to tell him, "Make a left!"

"Ok, I'll tell you, but you can't tell anybody. I mean, not a sole." He hesitated and looked back and noticed the headlights right on their tail. Damn near kissing their bumper, "I am a hitman."

"What! Get out of here!"

"Listen earlier I just killed a man. That's what I do. I kill for a living. Now take this gun, because tonight will be your first kill, so man up." He handed the pistol to him with the handle in his hand. He grabbed it by the handle and looked in the rearview mirror.

"Make a right! Make a right!" he told him. The sound of gunfire erupted, but the early morning dew had dampened the road. The car lost control and hit a ditch. It did not take long before all hell broke loose. The car landed in a muddy cow pasture. "We gotta get out of here, now! Let's go!" Mugumbi took the lead, despite the minor injuries; he grabbed him by the shirt, they made their way across the field to a barn. Kalargo was scared and he felt his legs weaken as he ran for his life. The ankle-deep mud slowed them but they used the cows as cover until they got to the barn.

"Hey stand here, I'll be over there. When I start shooting, I want you to hold your fire until I whistle. Then you let them have it." He walked away to the other side of the barn.

Kalargo stood in between a group of cows. He still remembered that stench and how his shoes were ruined. He remembered the cold chrome barrel that he rubbed against his forehead. How his hands shook because his mind told him he was going to die in a barn with cow shit on his damn shoes, before he could say a prayer, gunshots were fired from an automatic. The cows began to run. It was now or never. He started shooting after he heard the whistle. He shot two of the guys and Mugumbi shot and killed the other.

Kalargo ran over and kicked the mac-10 away from the hands of one of them. The other guy laid face up gagging and holding his throat. The bullet went through his neck. He stood there in shock.

"Well, what are you waiting on?" Mugumbi calmly approached, no fear or no sweat. His breathing was as if he had just woke up. The other survivor looked up at them with a bullet in his upper torso. The full moon lit the cloudless sky and provided enough light to see the eyes of this older man. "Well, it's your kill. You shot him. You finish him." Mugumbi walked over to the guy he shot and put another bullet in his head.

Kalargo looked at him and shook his head.

"Well, I thought I heard him breathe..." He frowned at him, "...just a little bit." His accent was stronger than his because he learned English later in life. Mugumbi walked over to him and stood behind him. "Listen..." he held Kalargo's arm up and aimed the pistol. "...Just." He spoke with a calm and relaxed voice, "...aim, and just pulled the trigger. Trust me, the last thing you need..." he whispered in his ear, "is to see this asshole again one day." He looked at his uncle and sighed. He quickly pulled the trigger four times. The nerves in his stomach were jumping like they were attached to a jackhammer.

He patted him on his back, "Welcome to a world that not many people have a chance to experience. Hey, it was self-defense. You can always tell your inner soul that, if that'll make you comfortable, at least I won't tell anyone."

He looked at his uncle and shoved the pistol into his pants.

"Look at it this way; you never have to kill him twice."

" Now I can live with that," Kalargo told him.

The taste of a bad grape reminded him that he was in his living room overlooking the pool through the French doors. He thought to himself, "Ten years went fast."

* * *

Later that evening

"Hello," Kalargo spoke into his cellular.

Jamie spoke over the music in the background. "Are you busy?"

"Of course not…" Kalargo said.

"We are going out to dinner at Nicholas Nicholas. Do you think you can meet us

there?" Jamie asked.

He was looking through his closet. "Sure I can. What time?"

"Ten thirty, I made reservations already. We'll see you there." They ended the call.

He entered his office and called Na Min. He sat at his desk with his feet propped on the edge of the two-inch-thick glass. "Annyong-haseyo…" Kalargo said.

Na Min was happy to hear from him, "Kalargo, I've been expecting your call. I've already transferred those funds. How did last night go? No problems?"

Kalargo slightly twisted his neck and spoke with confidence. "Of course not, you know how those last-minute decisions are handled." They both grinned a little. "How's Jamie doing?"

"Just fine, a matter of fact she and I are meeting tonight for dinner."

"She's a beautiful woman, I can see you and her being together for a very long time…" he quickly changed the subject, "…when was the last time you spoke to your uncle?"

He was surprised to be asked. "Actually I tried to call him today. But I got the answering machine."

"Have you heard about the store they opened?"

"What! He didn't tell me about that. That son of a gun, he's moving up in the world." He sighed.

"So that's the second store. The first one is in Osan, South Korea. Where is the…" before he could finish. "Yes, and the other store is in Pusan, South Korea. He and his wife…" he was interrupted.

"What, he tied the knot? After all these years…" he rubbed his left index finger across his eyebrow, "…he could have invited me." Kalargo sighed.

"Hey I don't mean to be rude but I'm a little busy. However, I wanted to tell you about the transfer, and to keep up the good work." Before he could end the call Kalargo asked him about the civil war in The Gambia.

"Everything's going accordingly, sometime this week we'll have to sit down

and discuss an important issue." he spoke with a more serious tone.

"If you are flying in from South Korea, it has to be important." He told him.

"Anyway, I'll give you a call. Until then, make sure you call your uncle." He agreed and they ended the call.

Kalargo flipped the switch on the computer and within minutes he was looking at his bank account. He transferred the funds to his business account, "Southern Pacific Martial Arts and Fitness" and most to a Swiss account. He smiled at the screen and decided to give his employees a bonus.

Moments later, the phone rang. "Hello."

The voice on the other end sounded muffled and echoed. "Hey, Kalargo…"

"Yeah, who is this?" Kalargo said. He looked down at the caller id and did not recognize the area code or country code.

"This is Crockett!"

"Heeey Crockett. Long time no hear, what's going on?" Kalargo asked before he could respond, "Where are you?"

He barely understood him. "I just arrived in Bahrain, a small island in the Persian Gulf."

"Wow, that big ship pulled into port?"

Crockett wiped his forehead of sweat. "No, actually we flew in from the carrier."

Kalargo leaned back and relaxed. "It's kind of hectic over in the Persian Gulf with Sadam acting a fool. You boys will be at war soon. What is it called, Desert Storm?"

"Yep, but I'm lucky I'll be in Bahrain, fifty miles from Saudi Arabia and three hundred miles from Kuwait." He stood in a small red phone booth.

"I know you wish you were back in Hawaii or at the least the Philippines?" Kalargo asked. "You have no idea how long you'll be over there?"

"It's no telling, maybe six months."

"Well…" he was interrupted.

"I might see you when I pass through for the martial arts competition in the Philippines."

"Well, I'm not sure if I will fly back or go back by ship. I would hate to miss a port of call in Australia." The phone booth was like a lava pit. "I've been here for five days and haven't seen a woman yet. They are all wrapped up"

They both laughed. "Hey be happy you're not in Afghanistan where they are covered from head to toe, and if caught staring too long is considered stalking." They laughed hard.

"Well, I am guilty as hell. Listen I have to go, I am running out of minutes." he quickly said. "When I get out I was thinking about working for you. You know once I get out of the military. It's time to make some real money. But we…" The female voice interrupted his conversation to advise him of his remaining seconds.

"Hey, you just keep your head low. The most important thing is making it back. I'll always have a place for you ok, but next time call me collect." They both agreed and ended the call.

Chapter Six

Kalargo grabbed his keys and walked out the door. He wore a black Giovanni Versace suit with a white button-up shirt. He looked his Lexus over for dirt. He sat in the driver's seat and pushed the number three for his theme song, "Pay Back" by James Brown. He looked in the rearview mirror to make sure his face was clear of shameful objects. He opened the armrest and lifted a bottle of Available by All Means cologne. He turned up the music and drove to Nicholas Nicholas.

It was a Tuesday night with a slight breeze from the east with clear skies. He arrived at the hotel that hosted the restaurant on the thirty-second floor. He pulled up to the valet and the attendant gave him a ticket, exited, and casually walked into the hotel. Before he could push the button, a couple entered the elevator, obviously drunk and having a good time.

"What floor?"

"Fifteen please." She said.

Her breast was literally falling out of her non-supportive dress. He looked away and pushed fifteen on the panel. "Sorry." The female said as they stumbled out on the fifteenth floor. Her dark brunette hair with a small number of gray strings gave her a Spanish look. He guessed that she had to be at least forty-five years old. Her earrings were studded with diamonds that matched her bracelet. He sighed with a smile and pushed the button.

He rubbed his mustache and eyebrows as he looked in the elevator mirror. As each floor passed the sound of the bell would ding, twenty-one, twenty-two, etc.

Finally, the elevator opened on the thirty-second floor and the skyline of Waikiki was a burst of city lights, it was beautiful. The live band can be heard. The candles that lit each table gave a welcoming feeling.

The host welcomed him. "Mr. Choi, your party awaits you. How is everything?"

He was known here like it was a second home, "Just fine, and you Steve?" Before he could respond, Jamie walked over and gave him a hug and a kiss. "We have a table by the window," she told him as they approached this white and burgundy-clothed table. Her friend was a gorgeous knockout blonde. She stood and greeted him. The waiter spoke to him, "I just started my shift. You enjoy. Your waiter will be with you shortly, drinks?"

He pulled his seat out and slowly sat down. "Give me a wine cooler, with the lemon flavor."

"Ladies and you're having?" Steve asked.

"I'll have a glass of your house wine," Jamie ordered, Stacy requested the same.

"So, this is Stacy the world has been talking about." He reached over to shake her hand, "…and I am Kalargo. I hope Jamie has told you all the good things about me." He smiled; his African accent can be heard a little on certain words.

"I've heard so much about you." She said.

He grunted, "I'm an ok type of guy."

She leaned forward. Her long hair was pinned up in a bun, but a small portion was in her face, using her thumbs to separate and push it behind her ears. Her lips were lined with a pencil. She was like a Barbie that had walked out of the Barbie doll factory. Her deep cleavage allowed her breast to rest on the table, not that he was starring, but, hey they were actually starting to talk to him.

"I…" She paused.

"And here are your drinks." The waiter placed them on the table, "Would you like to order or do you need more time?"

They looked at each other and agreed for more time. The waiter quickly walked away.

"Listen she was trying to tell me how you, how can I say it. Came here from Africa, is it true?" she looked him in his eyes.

Jamie interrupted, "Girl he doesn't want to talk about that stuff. Those were painful memories."

"Were they? I mean if you choose not to talk about it I would totally understand." Stacy said with a humbled voice.

He leaned forward and held Jamie's hand, "Well…" He looked her in the eyes. "There is something that I have not told anyone." He sighed and swallowed air. "I tell you what. Let's order and then I'll tell you how I and my uncle made our journey." He said as he looked over the menu. They agreed.

Stacy had to be no more than 5'8, a hundred thirty-five pounds, straight blonde hair that came to the middle of her back, thirty-eight, Double D breast, and her lips were glossy and kissable. She wore a satin dress that came two inches above her knees. Her tan was perfect. All of Stacy's gestures said to come home with me, not next week, or next month but right now.

"Is this your first time in Hawaii?" Kalargo looked at Stacy.

"Yes, she has been trying to have me visit her for years." She looked out of the huge picture window at the skyline. "It's so beautiful and scenic. I should have come a long time ago." She sighed.

"Girl, it took this long to get you here, now I hope it won't take the same amount of time to convince you to stay." Jamie grabbed her hand and they both smiled.

He thought that they were mighty touchy and clingy, but that's how females are in America he told himself.

"What do you think about her staying in Hawaii?" Jamie asked him.

He had to quickly pull his tongue out of Stacy's panties. He frowned. "Why not... I." He paused. "I'll leave it up to you guys. It is kind of expensive to live here." He sighed. "But..." He frowned and touched his mustache. "...I 'm sure she'll find work..." He was interrupted.

The waiter accosted the table. "Hello..." He stood with his hands behind his back. "Are you guys ready to order yet?" He asked with a patient but a feminine voice and gesture.

Kalargo rubbed his stomach.

"Hmm, yes I would say we are ready. I'll have whatever the special is." He looked at them to confirm.

They ordered their food while he patiently wrote everything down. He repeated their order and asked, "Anything else you would like to add?"

They were sure they had everything. He sighed and closed his eyes, rubbing the back of his neck. He took a swallow of his wine. Jamie and Stacy waited for this amazing story of survival.

"Ok, Africa, well I was born in a small village and from my understanding. My whole family was killed. The village was burned to the ground. My uncle took me from The Gambia, Africa to South Africa and worked in a diamond mine. He was later laid off and found work at the port loading cargo."Thinking of these events had his eyes pinkish red, tearful and increased his heartbeat. He sighed and continued. "Well…" He decided to skip a portion; "It was so many years ago, I had to be, what, nine?" He put his hands together in front of his face, rested his chin between his thumb and the bottom of his index finger. He told an intriguing story.

It was the early 70's

"Kalargo, you see that crate…" Mugumbi asked, "…You have to get inside, it's the only way we can go to America."

"I stood on the pier behind six-foot crates stacked on top of each other. A small number of people were working at three o'clock in the morning but the crowd had not arrived." He swallowed a good portion of his wine to remove the itchy sandpaper feeling that lay at the bottom of his throat.

"I'm scared." I told him, "He grabbed me by my shirt and yanked me towards him." He paused. "You listen to me. This is not the time to be scared! This is our only chance to get out of here!" He spoke with passion. His gestures were almost vivid. His hands were in front of him just as if he had taken the place of his uncle. "If we get caught trying to travel as a stowaway. We will regret it for the rest of our lives!" Mugumbi's hard whisper vibrated his ears. "For six months I've been

63

planning this trip. There is no time to horse around. Now crawl in!" He demanded.

He gently placed his hands on the table. Stacy and Jamie were totally blown away. The music by the band was tuned out. He had them by their ears like kids that were in trouble. Their eyes were fixed on his lips. He took a moment to look them in their wet eyes. He had noticed that they both were in shock and scared for his ordeal, but could not wait for what would happen next.

"Duck down! Shhh…" They quickly hid behind a wall of crates. A worker walked by, "Listen Tipi, These crates are next to be loaded, we have to do this now!" The look on Mugumbi's face was like the eyes of a lion, a mad pissed-off lion.

"I crawled in and he told me, now listen, whatever you do. Don't panic! You see these holes. Use them for breathing. I will come looking for you in four hours. He knew the order of loading. My crate will be on top. I'll come and get you out." He told me.

He gave me my travel bag that had food. He closed the crate. It was dark and scary. The heat was unbearable. The stench made me vomit so much I gave up on trying to hold it in. I was in this motionless position that had paralyzed me."

"I cried when I felt the crane lift the crate into the air. I felt like a caged animal. I held on to my bag and closed my eyes. For the first time, I told God that I was scared and I asked him to watch over me. I went to sleep."

Jamic and Stacy were so into his story. They forgot all about their drinks.

"I mean, of course, I trusted him with my life, besides, he did most of the loading on the pier. So I had no reason not to believe what he was telling me." He rubbed his face with his hands and shook his head. He scratched the back of his neck and leaned back into the chair. He was exhausted. The story brought back memories; the kind that would make a kid wet his pants. His voice was lowered. "We were in those crates for three days!" He whispered like a kitten's meow. He held his hands together in a praying form. His humbled voice could reach out and touch anyone's heart. He sighed. "I was seasick two different times. The Indian Ocean truly has no mercy on a weak stomach." He rubbed his stomach. "I heard a voice calling me. Tipi, are you OK?" I was weak. My lips were dry, too weak to respond, my uncle opened the crate. He threw water on my face. I was so thirsty; I tried to lick my forehead." He smiled but he was serious. "I almost died. He lifted my hand and told me we made it. We are here." He told me. He gave me some food that he had gotten out of the garbage. Damn it was good to have something, anything. I can't tell you what it was. It was all mixed up with other food that was tossed out. But I know it was fresh because it warmed my palms as I ate it out of my hands." He folded his lips inward and continued his story.

"When the ship docked in South Korea…" their eyes and mouth opened wider, "… yes, I said South Korea." He gasped for air and the girls swallowed his pain. "Because my uncle couldn't read, he assumed that the ship was going to America..." He leaned forward and looked them directly in their eyes, "...and we damn sure didn't speak Korean!"

"What the hell happened?" Somehow Stacy asked without moving her lips.

"Well the ship had an American flag on it, but it went to..." He had this look of surprise. "South Korea." Their mouths were literally on the table. "No way!" they looked at each other.

"My legs were numb. I was wet from urine and defecation. The smell of just me was enough to commit suicide. I was out of food after my third day. As far as being thirsty, I drank whatever I had to drink, and yes my own urine." He frowned, "Somehow my uncle thought it took four days to get to America." He laughed.

They both slithered their tongues out in disgust. Jamie wiped her eyes with the back of her hand. She carefully tried not to smear her makeup.

"I couldn't do it..." Stacy said.

He interrupted her. "Trust me; never say what you won't do." He waved his left index finger in front of them. "I thank God my uncle made me drink water for three days straight before our trip. I just can't imagine..." He paused. He was going to continue but the waiter had delivered their food.

"OK, you ordered the house special, all three of you. " His female-like voice was distinctive. He also thought Kalargo was handsome. He placed the plates on the table. The steam from the food can be seen.

Jamie looked at her plate and said, "Excuse me, hmm. What in the world is this?" She looked cute and timid as her curiosity gave suspicion. The waiter smiled and batted his lightly lined eyes.

"That is squid covered with a lightly marinated peanut butter, a splash of lemon, and on the side. You have garlic bread and pasta with a buttered squid sauce." He stood with his hands behind his back.

"Have you tried this? "Stacy asked him.

"No, but I heard it's good and very healthy." He paused. "If you have found it, not what you want, I'll be more than happy to replace it. No problem." They agreed.

Kalargo quickly mixed his squid into his pasta and commenced to chow down on his food. "Now this is good." He added more seasoning and squeezed a tab bit of lemon, with his mouth filled to his gills, he said, "I remember the first time I had this." He used the table napkin to wipe his lips. "I had to be… what ten years old. It's a Korean dish that is usually served as a celebration, but now a day, it's more or less a regular meal."

He held the fork in his right hand and pointed it at their plate. "But, you do have to acquire a taste for it." He smiled. It was at this moment Stacy was overwhelmed by this burning desire to have sex with him. She liked how his broken English rolled off his lips, and how intelligent he is. He knew so much about other places. He was so intriguing. Her eyes were wet, but her panties were wetter, she cried and wiped her eyes. She knew it would never happen. He just didn't seem like that type of guy, someone that would understand her.

At the end of their dinner, they rubbed their bellies and declared themselves full.

"Not bad, for a plate of, whatever it was." She smiled and pushed her plate away. Stacy looked at Jamie. "You still wanted to see his house?" she asked her before she could respond he raised his hand like a child in grade school that had an answer to a question,

"Check, please. Oh yeah, you wanted to see my house? It's OK." He said as he pushed his shoulders up. "I have to return for something anyway." He thought about her and how she's been playing footsie under the table with him. In his mind, he had to ask himself 'what kind of a friend is she? She just met me, and now, flirting with me?' He thought all of it was strange.

Later, they arrived at his house, the touch of a button, his double iron gates opened. Stacy's eyes open wide. "Wow…" she looked out the window like a kid's first time at Disney World and all the cartoon characters were lined up to meet her. This is gorgeous and wondered how he could afford such a luxurious place. Like a tour guide, Jamie explained the designs and culture behind the architecture.

"As you can see how fond he is of the Oriental culture…" She pointed out the native plants from South Korea, arches, and Buddha. "Now whatever you do…" they closed the doors to the car. "Don't step on his rose garden." Stacy carefully made sure not to. After showing Stacy around Jamie pulled him into the bathroom. "I know what you are thinking and she's not your type." She smiled as she rubbed her right hand over his zipper. She slowly unzipped his pants and pulled out his penis. He chuckled and looked directly in her eyes. His thumb slowly and lightly touched her forehead. She sat on the toilet and put his python in her mouth.

Suddenly, there was a knock at the door. "Jamie, where is the T.V. and entertainment you told me about, from behind the door his soft voice said, "She's busy. But the remote, that's on the coffee table, pushes the second red button." A brief pause before he could catch his breath. He combed his fingers through her hair, "Yeah, just push the red button and aim it at the wall across from the couch.

Stacy put her ear to the bathroom door, giggled with her hands over her mouth, and tiptoed away. The red button produced an entertainment center from the floor and she was entertained.

Moments later, Jamie entered the living room with a smile, "Girl…" Stacy put her hands over her mouth. "Shhh… I don't want to hear it." They both laughed.

"Jamie, where did you find this man?" Stacy looked at her with this curious look. Her lips tooted up as she tilted her head.

Jamie flopped onto the couch, crossed her legs and signed.

"You could have at least tried to brush your hair and wiped a little lipstick on or something." They both giggled like teens. Stacy leaned over, "What does he do?" She asked with curiosity.

The phone rang. "Do you want me to get that?" Jamie asked.

Kalargo's voice came from behind the bedroom door. "I got it! Hello."

The voice on the receiver was deep and troubled.

"Kalargo, the warehouse was raided!" Bennett said.

"What! Who all was arrested?" Kalargo asked.

He sounded like he was almost out of breath. "Pat, Damion, and big Mike. I have just left and I'll be damn…" He paused.

"Do you know who raided?"

"Honolulu police, it looked like they were looking for drugs. You need to call the dock!" He said.

"Who is the weakest link of them all?"

Bennett paused, "Damion."

"Well, get the lawyer and bail them all out, make sure you bail Damion out first. Was anything left behind?"

"No."

"But if they interrogate Damion long enough. They might find out that it's on the dock and the answer to your question, everything was already taken to the dock."

"I'll call you back. I got to call the dock." The phone call ended.

He slammed his fist down on the desk, "Shit." He dialed captain Tomzack's number nervously. After the phone call, he sat on the edge of the desk with his head in his palms. His buzz from the alcohol slowly drifted away. He heard the music coming from the living room. He thought of Stacy's tits and ass. "Hey." He rose up and threw on a pair of jeans. He applied green apple lotion and a small amount of Hugo Boss cologne on his chocolicious body.

"Sorry for being a horrible host." He walked out barefooted. Stacy's legs were slightly open.

"Jamie, you didn't offer her anything?"

"We were just sitting here thumbing through the music and talking about old times."

He walked over to the wet bar. "Let me see… I have Cognac, white wine or Vodka."

Jamie immediately said, "I'll have some white wine. Do you have any strawberries or grapes?"

Stacy boldly requested, "I'll have the bottle of cognac." She let out a strong sigh that lifted her small strands of hair from the front of her face.

He thought if she drinks this bottle, it's over. The freak will for sure come out tonight, he spoke beneath his breath. I'll have her stripping and eating Jamie's crotch and sucking me like a drunken vacuum." He continued to speak to himself. "My God, it's going to be a fabulous night and Jamie, she'll be too drunk to remember anything." He smiled.

"Ladies..." He gave them a glass and began pouring Jamie's drink first. Stacy quickly grabbed the cognac bottle, popped the cork, and slammed the mouth of the bottle like she had deep throated before. His eyes opened wide.

"Oh my..." He looked at Jamie. "You might need to keep an eye on her." He said with a sarcastic voice. He turned up the music and told them he'll be back. He slipped into his office. He sighed and used his palms to push the stress from his eyes to his ears and to the back of his neck. "I got to call Na Min..." He held the phone in his left hand and sighed.

"This is going to be harder than I thought" He pushed the first number. "If I do it now, I won't be interrupted later."

"Good evening," Na Min answered the phone. They spoke in Korean. He let him know that it was a small matter and it was nothing to worry about. Their conversation ended.

He returned to the living room. "Surprise, I am back." He stopped dead in his tracks. The bottle of cognac that was full was now half full. He pretended like he didn't see it.

They were laughing from the top of their gills. They had tears rolling down their faces. The wildlife channel showed a rare monkey encounter with a female monkey. The Japanese monkeys were in a cage. When the monkeys are having sex, the jealous male monkeys attack the male while he's having sex, knowing that he won't stop having sex until he has an orgasm. They immediately run when they are finished. The zoo doctors said that this is the only time they have an advantage in fighting this male monkey. He flopped down between them and laughed as he had never seen it before. Jamie leaned on him putting her right hand on his stomach. Stacy laughed so hard at the monkey's facial expressions until tears fell. Her legs were open and rubbing against his.

The monkeys yanked on his tail, punched, and vigorously pulled his facial hair. He looked so pissed off, but like usual he didn't stop.

Stacy grabbed the bottle of cognac and took a huge gulp. At the same time, Jamie looked at him, "Don't pay her any attention."

She held her stomach to reduce the pain that her laugh gave her. She stood and laughed her way to the kitchen, obviously drunk.

"Why is your kitchen moving so much?" She asked.

Jamie looked at him, "Nope… don't think about it."

For some reason no matter how idiotic she looked. She looked hot as hell. Suddenly the phone rang, "Thank God." Jamie said.

After three rings he had not moved, "Go ahead and get the phone… tell them I'm not here."

She picked up the phone, "Hello…" She looked at him. "It sounds very important." She handed him the receiver.

"I'll take it in the office." He grunted like a kid.

Jamie walked over to her, "Why are you trying to lead him on?"

Her eyes were bloodshot red and the fresh smell of cognac on her breath. She slowly and carefully leaned forward. "You told me…" Jamie was interrupted. Stacy softly placed her index over her lips. "I am just having fun." She held onto Jamie for support. "I really don't mean any harm." She struggled to return to the coach. Her words drooled off her lips, "Jamie…" her eyes filled with tears. "Why can't I find me a man like you?" She slowly shook her head and scratched her neck. Jamie laid her down on the couch. "No harm intended, you know everyone tells me that I am so beautiful, but I can't keep a man." She reached for the bottle. Jamie pulled her hand away. "No… I think you've had enough of that. Have you spoken to anyone about this?" Jamie asked her.

She looked her in the eyes; she softly bit her bottom lip. "Girl, it's been an ongoing nightmare." She used her left pinky finger to dig into her right ear. "Did I ever tell you how jealous I was of you? Ever since we were kids… I think I was cursed." She pushed her tears back and buried her face into the pillow. Jamie began to emotionally break down. Her best friend in the world is deeply depressed. She gave her a hug. They both burst into tears. She grabbed her hands and brought them to her face. "Stacy, you have to stay strong!"

"I know, but it's so hard!" Stacy whispered. "And no one understands." She looked Jamie in her eyes and grunted. "I am fucked up." She said.

Jamie stopped her. "No, you are my friend. You are Stacy." They both laughed and kissed each other on the lips.

Kalargo came from the room partially dressed, "Ladies... I'll be right back."

Jamie rose from the couch and walked over to him. "Is everything OK?"

"Yeah..."

She looked over her shoulder as she walked him to the door.

"I just have to take care of something. I'll be back." He gave her a passionate kiss on her lips and held her tight.

"I apologize for Stacy." She said.

He wedged his lips between hers and French kissed her. He inhaled her breath with his eyes closed. "If I ever wanted a best friend, it would be you." He held her hand as he walked to the door. She leaned her head in his upper arm. It was at this moment that he had realized how he truly felt for her.

"Put Stacy in the guest room." He opened the door. "When I get back, I want you in your birthday suit." They giggled and kissed each other goodbye.

Chapter Seven

Seoul, South Korea

Agent Na Min Choi sat at his desk. His diamond channel set pinky ring sparkled when he reached for the phone. He dialed his stepdaughter's home and waited for someone to answer. His old fashion reading glasses sat at the lower tip of his nose, his beige robe with gold initials, "NC". It was early in the morning, but this call was important. His stepdaughter answered in Korean. "Annyong-haseyo"

"Hello Yuki, don't mean to call you so late…" he was interrupted.

"Daddy, I was thinking of you earlier today. How is everything?"

He sighed, "Well…" He never discusses his business with her and she totally understands.

"Let's say a little hectic." He paused as if he had a lot on his mind.

"Your work is going to kill you; it's time for you to retire." Her words melted the wax in his ears. "Yeah in another five years." But she knew he could afford to retire now but he was in too deep. She looked over at Mugumbi, "Well I am sure if you are calling this late, you must be calling for Mugumbi." She heard his sigh, "I love you, my dear."

"Yes, I know." She gave the phone to her husband. "Honey, it's my dad."

Na Min tapped the tip of his fingers on the calendar that covered his desk. It was seconds before Mugumbi cleared his throat with his face half-buried into the pillow. His Korean was horrible in the morning hours, day hours, and whenever he tried to speak Korean, "Annyong-haseyo."

Whenever he called for business their dialogue was always coded to their understanding. "I am inviting you to the next executive party." His voice was calm.

Mugumbi looked at the clock, "OK."

"I know this is bad timing, but I need you on the next flight to Hawaii. You will have more details once you get there." Na Min circled a date on his calendar.

"Next flight?" He sighed. "Not a problem." Mugumbi closed his eyes.

At the age of forty-seven, he felt like a thirty-year-old, fit, healthy, but his downfall is his addiction. So far it has not yet interfered with his work. He used his left thumb to snatch an annoying nose hair. He looked at it.

"Is everything else OK?" Na Min asked.

"Oh yeah, I can't complain. Listen, I will call you when I touch down on the island." The line ended.

Na Min removed his glasses, grabbed his bottle of Gin, and thought about the first time he met Ginnifer. He looked at the glass and asked, "I no longer wonder how you have become my best friend?" Of course, she did not respond. He liked that about her. She gave him no lip, no limit to her love, and most of all, she had given him plenty of nights of satisfaction, and someone to talk to. She relieved him of bad dreams of those unspeakable acts to humans in the name of national security. Sometimes their faces haunted him in his sleep. He knew he could tell her his deepest secrets without her going around blabbing his business and getting him in trouble. He also knew that Ginnifer was slowly killing him. His liver was not functioning properly. He picked up his glass of Gin and slowly let the rim touch his lips. He kissed the edge of the shot glass and licked the rim. It was cold, he tilted it just enough to sip her wetness. She was warm and soaking wet, the no longer burning of his throat made their bond stronger. He looked at the glass.

"Am I an alcoholic, nope? Not, I say, Ginnifer." Na Min grinned.

He twisted the shot glass and poured it into his mouth like he was doing something super special. His tongue was relieved, his throat burned just enough to remind him of their bond, but not like it used to. Her strength was no longer potent.

"Am I losing my love for her?" He asked himself, "Ginnifer?" He tilted his head to the left, raised his voice, and looked at the glass and then the bottle.

"Now you know, you and I go way back. We can talk about anything." He tilted his head like she was naughtier than he. "You are not satisfying me like you used to. Is there anything that you would like to tell me?" He examined the bottle to make sure he had not substituted her for a cheaper whore in a bottle form. He knew she would not have liked that. "Never." He poured another shot.

Suddenly his wife knocked at the door. "Is everything OK?" She peeked in on him trying to make love to Ginnifer. He was caught in the act. She once told him that she was no good for him. He looked at her. "Just finishing my dear, I'll be to bed soon, just cleansing my breath." He quickly downed Ginnifer one last time for the night and tucked the Gin bottle in his cabinet behind him. "You know what?" He whispered to the bottle of Gin, "She has been jealous of you for years." And finally, he cut the desk light off. "Good night, see you next time."

* * *

Honolulu, Hawaii

Kalargo's car cruised smoothly on the highway at eighty miles per hour. He was tempted to go faster, but he was the only driver on the road at two forty-five in the morning. He slowed down to fifty-five; he received a call from an old friend that suggested that he meet him at the cafe off the highway. Even though he had not seen him in a while, he felt like he had always been trustworthy, so why not?

The cafe was practically empty and spooky under the circumstances he parked and entered. He sighed as he sat at the counter. The waitress asked, "Need a menu?" She reached for the menu.

He stopped her, "No, just a cup of coffee please." He looked around while he waited. He stretched.

"Sugar?"

"Ummm, yeah, and milk."

The waitress gave him a spoon and a napkin and went to get cream. He used the napkin to clean up, but he noticed some writing on the other side. He flipped it over. He thought it was very strange, he found it to be strange because it was in Chinese. He quickly looked around. He read it, "Someone is dirty among your crew. You need to clean house immediately!"

His eyes opened wide. He stood up and tossed two dollars on the counter and stormed out of the café, "Too spooky." He felt as he jumped in the car and sped off.

On the way home, he thought about each and every guy that worked for him in the past and to this date. He smiled because Stacy kept popping up on his mind, but he knew he had to focus.

Moments later, he arrived at his house. He tiptoed through the living room. The TV on, he cut it off. The guest room door was open, he closed it. He quietly crawled in bed like a sneaky snake. Jamie was sound asleep, naked, beautiful, and desirable. She was awakened by his wet tongue on her ankle and up her calf. She smiled and played like she was sleeping. He knew how to wake her up and he did it very well. They made love multiple times before falling asleep.

The next morning sun slowly moved between the shades and across Stacy's face.

"Ahhh…" She moaned.

"My head," it pounded like a bass drum as she lay in bed on her back holding her head, "I must have had way too much to drink." She lifted the sheets. She never got out of her clothes.

"I can't handle anymore of these wild nights." She mumbled, looked around, and realized that she was still at Kalargo's house. She was in the bathroom when she overheard Jamie and him making love. She leaned over the sink and sighed. She was sad deep down inside. She couldn't have a relationship that lasted more than two or three weeks. The relationship would end the first night of copulation. She buried her face in her palms and sucked up her depression, letting out an aggravating sigh of relief. She had learned to ignore her feelings and move on with life.

Kalargo sat behind Jamie in the Jacuzzi bubbled with strawberry suds. He slowly washed, massaged, and combed through her hair with his fingers. The shampoo lathered as he used more of it to wash and massage her back. He kissed her on the back of her neck. She leaned back and rested on his chest. She turned around and kissed him on the lips.

"I wish I could lie here all day." She put one leg out of the Jacuzzi. Suddenly she submerged herself and stood up, "but I know I can't." Her glossy body stood before him. She tiptoed into the shower to wash her hair of shampoo.

Moments later he remembered the napkin. He raised himself from the water and nakedly walked into the bedroom. His wet footprints trailed his every move. The soap suds slowly slid down his shiny wet body. He grabbed his pants from the dirty clothes hamper.

"Damn." He read it again, "Someone is dirty among your crew. Clean up the coffee spill, he has priors." He stood there thinking, naked as a jaybird. His wet hands soaked the napkin. He looked up at the ceiling.

"Need a towel?" He looked around as the towel landed on his shoulder. He wrapped it around his neck. He walked over to the nightstand, grabbed a lighter, and thought about burning the napkin.

He pulled his pants up to his legs and grabbed a white t-shirt. With the phone receiver in his hand, he dialed Bennett's number.

"Yeah, hello."

"Hey Bennett, wake up!" He commanded.

"I am awake."

"What happened last night?" He walked into the bathroom to brush his teeth.

"I did exactly what you told me. I bailed Damion out, and I am going to bail the others out right now." He paused, "What time is it?"

"Twelve thirty." He spoke with a mouth full of toothpaste and a toothbrush in his hand.

"Hold on." He could hear him coughing and clearing his throat and chest. "Babe, get up and get breakfast going. It's going to be another long day." Bennett told his wife in the background, "Yeah I'm back, now Damion, seems to be cool. He didn't say anything and they didn't ask him much either." He took a drag from his cigarette, "You know Kalargo, I think they knew he was a new guy, a truck driver that picked up and delivered. You know what I mean?"

"Hmmm, yeah." He gargled and spat out toothpaste and mouthwash. He thought about telling him about the napkin. "How did they know about the warehouse?" There was silence.

"No idea, the only reason I got away. I was standing by the escape tunnel." There was a pause and a question. "So what's next Kalargo?"

He walked out of the bathroom, "Hmmm, go bail out the other two; afterward, make sure you bring them both to me. At the same time, I got some checking around to do.", before he ended the call, "oh yeah, Bennett! Make sure." He repeated himself, "Make sure that you are not followed. They may put a tail on them." They both agreed. "Bring them to Burger King on Nue Nue st." The call ended.

As he placed the phone down, He could hear the TV and stereo on from the living room. He knew Jamie was in the closet getting dressed.

83

"Jamie, go and ask Stacy if she's going to eat breakfast. If not…" He reached for his shoes. "Are you hungry?" He asked her.

She exited the closet with a pair of jean shorts, "We are going to get a bite to eat, how do these look?"

He looked over his shoulder as he dug into the drawer for socks, "Absolutely stunning."

She walked over and kissed him.

"Well, I guess I'll get something on the go." He said.

She grabbed her keys and purse, "I'll call you later." She left with Stacy.

* * *

The sun beamed through Kalargo's windshield as he kept a paranoid eye on the inmate release at the Honolulu jail. He parked a block away to make sure Bennett was not followed. The first thirty minutes were crucial. He blasts the air condition hoping it would stop the trail of sweat that crawled down his back. He debated in his mind if he should take a chance of going to use the bathroom.

"Damn, I knew I should have used it before I left." He pushed down on his midsection and looked in his driver-side mirror. He grabbed a piece of gum and tossed it in his mouth and mumbled as he chewed his gum. He reclined his seat and adjusted his mirror. He sighed and nervously looked in all his mirrors and looked at his watch. "Five more minutes." He looked around and spotted a cafe that he could duck into to use the bathroom. He tapped his left foot against the bottom of the driver's door. "What the hell. I can run in and be out." He mumbled and opened the door. The sound of traffic and the smell of the downtown came to life. The exhaust of a cement truck slapped him as he dipped across the street and into the cafe. He weaved his way through the line.

"Excuse me, bathroom?" he pointed his finger.

"It's out of order." The employee said.

He rolled his eyes and turned around for the door. He stepped outside and immediately looked towards the jail. He walked funny, desperate, and noticed an alley across the street.

"Thank God!" He quickly held his hand up at the moving traffic to jaywalk, "Hey sorry." He waved at the driver. In the middle of the street was when he saw a patrolman watching him.

"Great, ahh no." he saw Bennett, Steve, and Pat shaking hands with the bondsman. He quickly turned around and rushed back to his car. He sighed. "Damn it! About time they come out!" He jumped in and cranks the car, blowing a bubble as he looked in the driver's mirror.

"Come on!" he inclined his seat.

He put his car in drive and just before he could drive off. The patrolman tapped on his window. He looked at him and signaled to roll down the window. He nearly pissed on himself.

"Shit. Shit. Shit." He slowly rested his head on the headrest.

"How can I help you Mr. Police officer?" He looked like he had piss up to his eyes.

The officer stepped back from the car.

He looked Samoan, big and well-tanned with curly short hair. He was very big, perhaps closer to fat and fighting to stay in his little brother's uniform. He looked very cultural. He smiled. He held his frown tightly. He held his pad in his hand and pulled his pen from his shirt.

Kalargo was tapping his foot nonstop.

"This is a fine automobile. Is this one of those new Lexus's LS400?"

He was in shock and a little pissed, "Yeah."

"Bro I like this car. I was thinking of getting my daughter one of these. You know for her graduation. How does it ride, pretty fast?"

Kalargo looked in his mirror, "Hmmm, Superfast" He anxiously said.

"I saw you earlier. You looked kind of lost."

"Well, I am a little lost. Do I make a left or right to get to the hospital?" He looked at Bennett's car drive by. He quickly answered his own question, "Now I remember, left and two blocks on the right." He looked up at the officer.

"You got it right." He noticed a car parking in front of a fire hydrant, "You have a nice day." He went from a fan to an officer of the law.

He followed Bennett trying to notice a tailing undercover car, nothing. "So far so good," he mumbled. It took thirty minutes to get to Burger King. He dialed Bennett's number.

"Bennett, what's going on?" He parked several blocks away after carefully driving around, "It's cool baby, just here waiting for you to call. I didn't think you would show." He sighed and sipped on a vanilla milkshake. "Well, what's going on?" He closed his car door and walked towards the Burger King.

"They have a court date."

"Who's the judge?" He waited for a response. He could hear him asking them in the background.

"Judge Kalani, does he ring a bell?"

"Well, let's just say thank God it's him." He laughed and sat down across the street from the Burger King and looked for anything out of the normal.

"Let's say he and my father are golfing buddies. We can take care of him."

He pulled a seat and thought about how crooked he is.

"I'll handle it from here. Everybody go home and wait for my call. I'll have the lawyers drop some names and get this thrown out."

* * *

Under clear blue western skies that were being chased by darkness from the east. The sun descended slowly. The purple and yellowish red eye danced on the horizon. The brightest stars can be seen as the flight from South Korea circles the island of Oahu.

"Ding ding." The fastened seat belt light illuminated. The captain's voice was calm over the intercom.

"Ladies and Gentlemen, I would like to welcome you to Honolulu, Hawaii. The weather is currently 89 degrees with a slight breeze out of the north. I hope you have enjoyed your flight to the south pacific islands of paradise. We should be landing in twenty-five minutes." The captain pointed out the different islands of Hawaii and a little bit of history about them.

Mugumbi stretched and lifted his blind to his window. He reached for the air plane's phone. He slid his credit card through the slot and started dialing. His Korean was warm to hear and his wife was excited to talk to him.

"Hello." She was still in bed.

"Just letting you know that the plane will be touching down soon."

She loved his accent in Korean, but she never knew it was the voice of a hitman.

"I love you." She said.

"I love you. I'll be back in a week, maybe sooner." He put his seat belt on.

"I'll be waiting." She gave him a kiss over the phone and they ended the call.

Chapter Eight

The sweat dripped from Kalargo's body as he strained to push 270 lbs off his chest. His veins were like roots from a three-hundred-year-old tree. He trembled as he slowly pushed the bar. He didn't have a spotter to help him. He found the inner strength and concentration to clear the stand. His heavy breathing pushed small amounts of sweat from around his lips, as he sat up and hung his head between his chests, resting his elbows on his upper thigh. He deeply planted his thumbs on his temples and massaged his headache, looked around his weight room, and sighed. He used his forearm to wipe his face. He was stunned.

"What the hell…" His forearm was smeared with blood. He ran over to the mirror. "Damn." He grabbed a towel. Lately, his nose bleeds, and headaches started to reoccur. He relaxed and held his head back with the towel on his nose. Before leaving he noticed CNN news was talking about the Persian Gulf and Iraq invasion of Kuwait.

"It's shameful how they focus on all of this oil. When there are many countries at war. But because they have nothing to truly contribute to the world…" He disappointingly shook his head. "…they are overlooked, thousands die without help, but then again this is sadly my way of making money." He walked into the living room.

He checked the towel for blood. "Someone has to help the poorest people in the world." He claimed. "They are sending five hundred thousand troops. For what, oil?" He sucked air between his beautiful white teeth. "I've sent ammo to over thirty countries that have been at war for more than five years, but no one jumped in to stop the mass killings in none of those countries." He checked his nose and grabbed a bottle of water.

"Yep, let them keep worrying about the powerful countries. I'll keep making my money." He said as he nodded his head at a shameful game the world plays. As he passed through the living room he pushed play to hear Anita Baker while he took a long hot bath. He lit the candles, ran the water, and plucked nose hairs. He applied his shaving cream.

* * *

"Room four fifty-five please." Mugumbi checked into his hotel. The receptionist gave him a key without question. "Enjoy your vacation." She smiled. She didn't know it, but she had just ruined his moment. He hated people that displayed a fake- smile. He nodded his head, "Thank you."

He found his room, slid his key, and opened the door. He looked in the bathroom, closets, and under the bed. Finally, he looked under the mattress and pulled a small black case that contained a .380 caliber revolver and silencer. He looked at his watch and walked over to the T.V. and turned it on. He scans the channels for his favorite South Korean program.

The United States seemed so different from him. He had grown accustomed to the South Korean way of life. However, Hawaii catered to Japanese tourists. "Found it." He always amazed Americans when he spoke Korean better than he spoke English. He entered the bathroom and looked in the mirror. He rubbed his fingers across his mustache, pushed his lip up to inspect his gums. He licked his lips to moisturize them. He looked down at his arm and touched his needle tracks. One by one he touched them like his temple had been destroyed. For the first time, he realized how ugly and embarrassing they were. He wore long sleeve shirts to hide them.

He spent some time in the bathroom. The hotel phone rang; he walked over to answer it, with his beloved dope in his right hand, and picked up the receiver with his left. He sat down on the bed and listened. Finally, he hung the receiver on the phone. He walked over to open the door. There was no one; he saw an exit door down the hall. He quickly grabbed his .380, loaded it, and slid it in his front right pocket. He ran towards the exit and hid. Behind the exit door, he peeped through the crack of the door. "Hmm..." he raised his eyebrows out of curiosity. He saw a twenty-five year old, short curly black hair, of Polynesian descent. He stopped in front of Mugumbi's hotel room door, without hesitation he pulled an eight by twelve mustard envelope from beneath his shirt and slid it beneath the door. He quickly ran down the hall and disappeared. For the first time, he actually saw who the messenger was. He made sure it was clear before coming from behind the exit door. In his room, he retrieved the envelope that contained a map, itinerary, photo, and directions to the location of his victim. He pulled the picture out and sat down at the desk. The light from the window entered that side of the room. He leaned forward, resting his elbows, and studied the picture. He wanted to remember as much as possible, like the scar beneath the bridge of his nose.

After an hour of preparation, he grabbed the receiver, and dialed 0, "Yes, this is the front desk of the Marriott Waikiki. How can I help you?"

"Yes, I would like to have a rental car to go sightseeing."

"Are you interested in a small, compact, or economy?"

He thought about it. "Do you have a four-door sedan?"

"I can check, give me one moment, please. Can you hold?"

"Yes." He held the photo in his hand.

"Yes we do, we have the Chrysler Cirrus." There was silence. He had no idea what the Chrysler Cirrus was, but it sounded good.

"Yeah, I'll be down to pick it up in thirty minutes." They both agreed and ended the call. He quickly primped and left the room.

He wanted to be as familiar with the area as much as possible and with the victim's daily movement. The target lived in a high-rise condo on Ala Wai Blvd, a busy one way that becomes quiet after one thirty in the morning. The canal that separated Waikiki from Honolulu had a golf course that stretched the length of the canal. He is a nocturnal creature of the night. His favorite place on the weekend is a popular club by the name of Candy Paint. He was known to be heavily drunk, and flamboyant.

He drove down the Blvd checking every alley, garbage dumpster, nook, and cranny. He looked for cameras, smoke areas, and parking garages. He looked at his watch. The hour hand was on the nine and the minute hand was slightly on the six. He pulled over to the right and grabbed his bag of bread to feed the ducks. He wanted to walk and learn the area. He may have to jump in the canal and run across the golf course to getaway. He wore a pair of navy blue loose-fitted cotton shorts, a brown golfer's wide brim hat, with sandals that buckle around his ankle. His gun was tucked between his belt in the back of his pants. He walked for two hours before he decided to walk to the club.

* * *

The next morning the sun rose between the mountains and played peek-a-boo with the clouds. Some parts of Honolulu were wet from passing showers. Mugumbi lay in bed tossing and turning from a dream. He spoke in his native tongue. He woke up reaching for his right thigh and realized there was a knock at the door. He sighed. His eyes opened as he heard the lock on the door opening.

"Room service."

"Good morning…" He quickly slid the gun in the pocket of his Marriott robe.

"Room service?" She asked.

"Hmm…" He stood and slowly asked for her to come in.

"It's not a problem, I could come back later if you prefer?" her timid manner and voice were cute. He walked over to the window and sat down holding his leg. He rubbed the scars that had not healed properly.

"You need ice on that?" The maid said as she entered the bathroom.

"No, it's not as bad as it looks." He walked over to remove his travel bag from the edge of the bed. "Lesson learned," he said to the maid.

She peeked from the bathroom. "Excuse me."

He felt like talking since she had seen him touching his leg.

"The scar, I said that it was a lesson learned." He opened the travel bag.

"And what was that?" She said and returned to cleaning the bathroom.

"The lesson learned was to always be careful with your enemies." He laughed and she didn't get it. He stuffed the eight-by-twelve envelope under his arm and walked out of the room.

When he returned, the room was cold, cleaned, and scented. He tossed his newspaper on the bed, unbuckled his belt, and pulled it from around his waist. He opened his needle kit and sat on the edge of the bed next to the nightstand. He put a small amount of water on his crooked-shaped spoon. Like a scientist, he carefully added his heroin to the water and heated the spoon with a lighter. The flames darken it black as the substance bubbled. From the spoon to the syringe he put it, quickly grabbed the belt, and tightened it around his upper bicep. He put the end of the belt in between his teeth to hold it. He pulled harder until his veins looked like a batch of muddy earthworms. He sighed as the rush of dope made its way through his body. He sat there thinking about the feeling, the warmth, and the love that followed.

* * *

Seoul, South Korea

In the eyes of a fifteen-inch goldfish that swam toward the glass of a beautiful fish tank. It looked forward to being fed. Na Min stood with food in his hand, "Here Topi, I don't know if I'm feeding you too much or too little." He tossed food in the tank; Topi swam to the top to gobble the crumbs.

He turned his back to the huge exotic fish tank that held some of the world's rarest fish. "Damn what's taking him so long to call me?" He looked at his watch. "He's late." He walked over to his desk to make a decision. He decided to wait for Zang's phone call, "Honey if the phone rings, take a message, I'll be …" He was interrupted by the phone, without hesitation. "Hello."

"Yeah, Na Min, I hope I didn't have you waiting?"Zang sighed. "We have a small problem," he paused.

"What kind of a problem?" Na Min asked.

There was silence and then a huge sigh that warmed his earpiece. "Well as you know we have invested a lot of money in this country. Our people are not, how can I say it? They don't quite fit in. They stand out like pink tigers."

Na Min sat down and tapped the eraser of his pencil on the desktop calendar. He broke the silence. "Other words, you would like to have, perhaps a black…" He swallowed his fear of his request. "…person." The tapping stopped and the pencil fell from his hand. He rubbed his thumb across his eyebrows and slowly pushed his hand to the back of his neck and massaged it. "Zang, I don't have anyone qualified with the military experience." He leaned back into the seat. "That is a lot to be asking for Zang. Do you know people are watching me? They are suspicious. Do you think I have people that I can just pluck from my hand for this kind of stuff?" He closed his eyes.

"Listen, we trust you and it's the only reason we are asking you. We trust your decisions and we are willing to make it worth your while." Zang said.

"Zang, you think you guys have all the answers. This year is supposed to be our final operation. But now you call me with all this. I don't know what to make of it. I mean, come on! What do you think, this is Zang?" He threw the pencil across the desk with anger, "I just can't believe this." He poured a glass of Gennifer and slammed it down his throat.

"Na Min, I swear we are planning to make this our final request for you. You have delivered throughout the years and you have had some close calls and hairy situations. We are willing to compensate you for everything you have done for us."

His breathing can slightly be heard; before he could speak he was interrupted.

"How would you like to mysteriously inherit a two million dollar apt building?" He waited for him to respond.

"How important is this, so call, black person? What do you need him to do?"

"Well, wc need someone who could go in undetected, speak the native language good enough to pass as one of their own, and we are willing to train him if we need to." He paused.

"And the mission of this person?" he knew he preferred not to talk about it.

"We need to give an executive party to General Kakambo Twigani."

He realized how heavy this was and the difference it would make to the war. The North Koreans were no longer trying to just make money from the diamonds and oil. They were trying to perhaps colonize and control this small African country.

The sound of the Gin came from the bottle as he poured another glass. "Zang, Zang, my God what are you trying to…" He held the receiver from his ear and choked it with his hands and gritted his teeth. He calmly put the receiver back to his ear. He sighed. He leaned forward and planted his elbows on the desk.

"How long before the drilling will begin for oil and diamonds?" He asked him.

"Well, that is a part of the problem. A lot of things can't get done unless the war is over, but, if we don't have control over the situation. One of the NATO countries will eventually step in and gain control and discover natural resources."

"How many apt buildings do you have?"

Zang grunted, "Plenty in the United States and in other countries."

"I tell you what. I want three apt buildings at ten million inherited to me." He said.

"So, this means you can deliver?" His desperate voice of urgency was slowly relieved.

"Listen, we will go over everything in greater detail." Na Min said.

"Hmm… We need someone soon, like in the next three weeks." He said with concern.

"Zang, relax and wait for my phone call." He ended the call.

* * *

Honolulu, Hi

It was nine-thirty and Mugumbi's mind was made up to where the hit would take place. He figured he would follow him and park down the street from the club. He looked in his rearview mirror, finally, he saw the black Benz pull out from the condominium.

"OK." He waited until he passed him, looking to verify the license plate number. "That is it."

After two hours, he was frustrated. The prospector stopped four different places before arriving at the club, he knew if allowed his frustration to get involved something could go wrong. It was one-thirty in the morning when they arrived at the club, now came the wait.

Chapter Nine

The parking garage of the club was located among a plaza of stores, three stories high and very spacious. "Ding, ding." The elevator door opened and the club customers giggled as they looked for their cars.

"I hope this is the right floor." She was obviously drunk and leaned on the shoulder of her girlfriend. Their voices echoed as the clacking of their hills tapped and scratched the concrete. The voices silenced as they walked further away from him. The sound of keys dangled and the laughter can barely be heard.

He looked at his watch and sighed. "It's almost about that time." He wiped a bead of sweat from his nose. His black golf gloves were skin tight. He also thought the garage could be a bad place to make this happen. The crowd continued to exit the elevator and walk to their cars. He ducked, a couple walked from the floor below searching for their car. The keys are heard opening the car door. Their lips locked with a French kiss. One thing leads to another, it did not take long for the windows to fog. She moaned softly but the movement of the car was inevitable.

"Ding ding." A group of people walked off the elevator. "Look!" They were in shock. "God, Oh my." They giggled as they stared at the couple and rushed toward their cars.

More people passed them and finally, they cranked their car up and left. Not many cars remained on this floor, and again the prospector took forever. Suddenly the elevator door opened and the man in the photo exited. He whistled, as he retrieved his keys from his pocket.

"Good nobody is around." faced down in front of the victim's car. He pulled out his gun and twisted the silencer on tightly. The echoes of his whistling stopped. Mugumbi's heart pounded his chest so hard it felt like it was in slow motion. He did not know if he had been seen or not, but it was an uncomfortable feeling. The victim stopped to where only his shoes could be seen. He appeared to be looking around. Finally, he slowly walked cautiously as if he was suspicious.

Just before he pulled the trigger, suddenly a car horn blasted the parking garage.

"Oh my God!" it startled him. A loud voice came from afar.

"Long time no see."

"Wow, Mr. Kobalulu. How long has it been? At the least, what? Five years." They hugged and spoke for a while. Their conversation was unintelligible. They laughed as they said their goodbyes.

"Come on." He waited for his friend to drive off, wet his lips, gripped the handle on his gun.

He inhaled deeply, closed his eyes, and listened to his footsteps. The sound of the car keys dangling. It was so quiet, peaceful, and sudden. The sound of the silencer was so vacuumed-like and just powerful. The victim fell over in his car.

"Perfect." He walked by and quickly closed the door with his hip. He looked around the garage and shook his head. He looked into the car and shot him two more times in the head to make sure he was dead and walked away unnoticed.

* * *

Kalargo covered his head with his pillow. The phone rang; he tried to ignore it by pushing a button on the nightstand to shut off the ringers on all the phones in the house. Ten minutes later, his cellular phone was ringing. He also turns it off as he mumbled and cussed, "It's probably Jamie."

Fifteen minutes later, his pager goes off, "God damn it!" he snatched his pager and looked at it. "No way…" he turned the phones on and dialed Mugumbi's number. They spoke in their native tongue, "…hey uncle. It has been a while. You picked a good time to call."

"Well I was in town for a couple of days, so I decided to visit my nephew."

He pulled the pillow over his face and looked at the clock. "Hmmm, it's ten in the morning." He swallowed a dry throat. "I needed to get up anyway." He gave him directions to where he lived.

Later that day

As Mugumbi walked out of Kalargo's house, Bennett walked up to the driveway.

"Uncle this is my number one guy, Bennett. This is my Uncle I always tell you about." They shook hands.

"South Korea, right yeah he speaks of you. It's a pleasure to meet you. Hey, I'll be inside." Bennett made his way in the house.

"Yeah go ahead."

After ten minutes Kalargo came in. "I got some information."

"What you got?" Bennett asked.

He pulled out a photo of Saul. "Do you recognize him?"

"Yeah, he used to work for me. Where did you…" before he could say another word, he showed him a note, "I found this on my windshield." He gave him the note.

"Wow." He gave him the note back and told him to wait a moment. He told him about the napkin from the café.

"What does it mean, you have a spill?" Bennett asked.

"Clean up the dirty spill, someone is dirty among you." They both looked at each other and shook their heads. Bennett rubbed his bottom lip with his left thumb and sighed.

"And he left out of the blue, no reason at all; you know what we have to do?" Kalargo looked at him. "This is the rat that had the warehouse raided." He grunted.

"How do you know?" Bennett wanted to be for sure.

Kalargo sat down to explain, "Check this out the same night the warehouse was raided. I received a phone call from an old friend of mine. He told me to meet him at the cafe. It was important. But when I got there, I waited, ordered coffee. Somehow, this note manages to come with my coffee. The waitress had no idea how it got there."

"So who is the old friend?" Bennett asked.

Kalargo's right index finger pointed toward the ceiling, "I can't say. If he went through this much trouble to let me know this. It would be best to keep him anonymous." They both agreed.

That was one of the good qualities that he liked about Bennett If he did not try to know more than what he needed to know.

"So this is the guy?"

"Got to be," Kalargo assured him.

"Are we sure?" Bennett looked at him.

"All of this can't be a coincidence."

"I guess he got it coming." Bennett sat down and sighed. "Just say when boss."

"Go ahead and go home, I'll call you later tonight when I get the address on this guy." Bennett stood and walked himself out

Later that night

Bennett opened the door of the Kalargo's old mustard green 1970 impala. The interior was dated, the rust on the outside made its way to the inside. The motor sounded like a sewing machine, but the overall appearance was downright ugly.

"Wow, you are really trying to be low-key, aren't you?" he laughed. "Where in the hell did you get this from?"

He smiled, "A guy at a junkyard. They were giving it away." before he could respond, "Hey, you have everything? I don't want to have to return for anything."

"Yep." He looked at his disguise, fake tattoo on his neck, curly hair wig, and beard. They both looked like they were flashback disco seventy kids.

"So where does he live?" Bennett asked.

"The other side of the island there is a small house in the middle of nowhere." He made a left turn as the sound of the blinker ended. "He lives by himself."

"So how do you want to do this?" Bennett scratched the back of the neck.

"I don't know but it depends on my feelings." He cracked the window to allow the highway wind to cool his scalp. He looked at the dashboard clock, and down between his legs were his black gloves. He grabbed one and used his right knee to steer the car at seventy miles an hour. He pulled the glove over his right hand and then the left.

"Go ahead and put your gloves on, I got this." He pointed at a bottle of general purpose cleaning spray," Go ahead and wipe down everything, that way if we have to run, our fingerprints won't be in the car."

That was one of the qualities he liked about Kalargo, he was smart, and on top of his game.

"If you have to sneeze, don't. But if you have to, do it on your sleeve, better yet, in your shirt." As he was talking Bennett pulled out a pack of cigarettes, "And if you have to smoke..." he paused and looked at him. "...swallow the butt of the cigarette."

"Yeah right..." He pulled out a cigarette and put it between his lips. He looked at him.

"That cigarette will get you one or the other, prison time, or killed."

Bennett slowly and unwillingly pulled the cigarette from his lips like a lollypop had been snatched from a kid. He looked out the window and looked at all the palms trees that started to look like long-haired cigarettes. He placed the cigarette above his ear. He sighed.

"Are you serious?" He asked him as the cigarette palm trees passed his window.

"DNA, it has sent more people to prison than any witness. Hey, we'll be there in five minutes."

The entry from the highway down this dark road was perfect. They parked the car and retrieved a bat, two pistols, and rope. The lights upstairs had just turned off. The television was the only visible thing. They both stood outside and planned how they would gain entry into the house.

"Are you sure that there isn't anyone home?" Bennett asked him as he slid the pistol into his right back pocket.

He sighed, "Well…" He scratched his head. "…if it is." He rubbed his nose with his left hand, "We can't leave any witnesses, but, it shouldn't be." He led the way towards the front door. Their voices were at a whisper. "On three, we kick the door in and run upstairs." They both nodded.

"One, two…" Before they counted to three, a person came down the stairs. It was him. They looked at each other. They started the count over.

The huge noise of the door crashing down, glass shattered everywhere scared Saul. He dropped his glass and before he could reach for a weapon. A pistol was on top of his upper lip.

"Don't move," Bennett said with a crooked smile. His mask covered his face, but his eyes stared him down. "You snitch ass motherfucka."

Saul tried to explain. "What!" His fat jiggled like an ornament on a windy day. His white shorts sagged, the sleeveless shirt revealed his hairy armpits, his chest hairs protruded out the v cut shirt. His huge feet looked stressed from the three hundred and ninety pound bodyweight that gave him a hard time breathing.

"Sit your ass down!" Kalargo said.

The table was behind him. A fresh cup of hazelnut coffee and a plate of ginger cookies sat untouched. He had returned to get his night snack.

"Man, what is this? What you want, money? Look I got money!" He pushed his shoulders upward like money was no problem.

Kalargo held his head back and let out a huge sigh of relief. From the bottom of his throat, he pulled off the mask.

Saul fell from the chair as he tried to crawl away from him. "Kalargo! What are you doing here?"

He walked around the table. Saul's eyes followed his every move. He tried to read his mind.

"Are these fresh?" He picked up the plate of cookies.

"Yeah, go ahead have some." He was so scared.

"I still can't think of a reason." Bennett stood between them both until Kalargo walked completely around and leaned on the outdated kitchen counter. He looked around and noticed how he was living.

He took a bite into one of the cookies and tossed the rest in his mouth.

"Oh my God, Did you bake these?" He tried to catch a fallen crumb.

"Bennett, you can take off the mask now. I know it's uncomfortable."

"Yeah" he pulled it off, "it's hot as hell in here." His sweat ran down his neck, fanning himself to cool off.

"Listen, this is not what you think it is. I can explain." He was interrupted.

"How long have you had this house?"

He looked puzzled. "Little over three years."

"Hey, Bennett you want a cookie?" He turned it down, "They don't make cookies like these in my home country, are you sure you baked these? You mean to tell me that there is no other person here?" Kalargo wiped his mouth with his forearm.

"I swear I baked them." Saul's breathing was in between his words.

Kalargo turned his back, "Now it's a shame that I had to come out here on this occasion." However, he turned around with his mouth filled with cookies, "Damn, I think I am addicted to these cookies." He held one cookie in his hand. He walked over to Saul.

"I know you didn't think I was going to hog all of the cookies did you?" He walked over to him. "I got two choices for you. Deed me the property and we could act as if this never happened."

Before he could finish, "Yeah anything Kalargo, whatever you want!" He begged him. His fat face gave him a sad clown look.

"Or you could give me the recipe for these cookies and maybe." He paused a minute. "Just maybe, we could work something out." Before he could finish, Saul fell to the floor like a struggling whale begging to go back out to sea. From his knees, he started yelling out the recipe.

"Shhhh, hey it's no way I could remember that, come on man." Kalargo was smiling.

"Hey sit back in the chair." It took him two minutes to climb his ass back into the chair that creaked and moaned that it may break into pieces any moment. He looked back at the counter at the plate. One cookie left. He reached for it, just before he bit it. He asked him if he wanted it. He hesitated, but he said yeah nervously. In the palm of the black glove was the last cookie.

"Milk?" he asked him. He nodded his head.

"Now I really did not come here to hear all these excuses. You understand me?" he cleared his nostrils, "Now you have two choices right?" Kalargo rubbed his nose with his right index "But out of those two, which one do you think I want?" He looked him dead in his eyes. The shape of the cookie can damn near be seen going down his throat.

"The house?" Saul looked at him.

Kalargo stood back and opened his eyes and hands as if he guessed the right answer. He pulled out some documents and told him to sign them. "So for what you have done. And you know…" He threw up his hands like it was obvious. I am going to punish you forever to be poor." He scratched his head.

Bennett looked at him like he was crazy.

Saul looked relieved. "So if I sign them, everything would be forgotten about?"

"Did you drink some milk?" He pointed at the milk.

Saul quickly grabbed the cup and drank it empty; milk spilled from his bottom lip and ran into the valley and creeks of his fat flaky rolls of caked-up dirt around his neck.

"Oh yeah, how much money do you have?" Kalargo paced the kitchen floor. He pulled down on the bottom of his gloves to tighten them.

"I have six hundred thousand under the staircase." He pointed to the key on the wall. "That's the key, the brown one."

He gave him the ink pen. "You did well, especially with the cookies."

"Bennett, keep an eye on him. I'll go check the staircase out."

It took him five minutes to pull out the huge duffel bags of money from the staircase. He walked back into the kitchen sweating like he had run a marathon.

"Jesus Christ, you were not lying." He looked at his watch. He knew he only had about five more minutes before the cyanide pill would kick in.

"Bennett, give me a hand with these bags."

"What about..." He started to ask.

He peeked into the kitchen, looked at Bennett, and then at Saul. He waved his hand and looked at his watch. "He'll be fine." He returned to the staircase.

They carried the two duffel bags to the car. They were breathing hard, sweating through their clothes. "Come on let's go." He told him.

The ride back was peaceful; Bennett reached over and turned the radio on. He sighed and pulled out a cigarette. He kept his mouth shut and waited for him to say something.

Kalargo looked in the mirror for any followers. "Bennett, when we get to where we are going, take one of the bags for yourself. But whatever you do. Don't let anyone know you got it." He looked at him. He agreed to it.

"Do me another favor, let the window down?" Bennett responded, "Not a problem."

Chapter Ten

"Listen!" Na Min vehemently said. "Your Honor, this warehouse is owned by the U.S. Navy, which is two miles down the road. Everything inside of it belongs to the training exercise that is top secret. The FBI had been given a bad lead. Yes! I do appreciate their duties and professionalism. However, bad information does not give them the right to confiscate, interfere with a government training exercise." He looked the federal judge directly into his eyes. "I really need you to look the other way, drop the case."

As they sat over a dinner that had not been touched, He slid an envelope that held an undisclosed amount of cash. "Done?" He held his hand on top of it.

The judge sighed; He quickly pulled the envelope from the table. He shook his head, "Consider it done."

He had learned a long time ago to always cover his own ass. As he walked out of the restaurant, he pulled from his coat pocket a digital voice recorder and turned it off. As he walked towards the street, he reached for his phone and dialed Kalargo's cell.

"Yes hello."

"Hold on, let me get off the other line." He clicked over to Jamie.

"Hey, Jamie, it's my father. I will call you after I talk to him." She pouted and he clicked over.

"Kalargo."

"Yes, I am here." He sighed and wondered what he wanted to talk to him about. He hoped that it had nothing to do with Saul's murder.

"Listen, I wanted to talk to you about a project that requires your caliber of expertise." Na Min paused.

Kalargo stood up and walked into his master suite. "Hmm, hold on. Is it anything like Jakarta?"

"Oh no, no, no nothing like Jakarta." He grinned.

"But it does. Hey, listen. I'm in Hawaii. Most of what I need to tell you. I prefer to speak to you in person. What are you doing in one hour?"

He looked at his watch, "That will be, ten-thirty." He sighed. "Where would you like to meet? You know you are always welcome to come over to my place." Kalargo suggested.

"You live too far, and it is late. I have a flight in the morning." He sighed. "Meet me at the bar that we always meet at. Say no later than ten forty-five." They agreed and the line ended.

He quickly called Jamie. "Hey…"

She was excited. "Wow, that was fast."

"We have a change in plans. My father is in Hawaii and he says he needs to speak to me in person. Hmmm, maybe I can meet you after I finish talking to him."

"Or maybe you could pick me up on your way to meet him. I'm sure he would be happy to see us together." She could hear it in his voice that it might not be a good idea.

"No, how about we meet at eleven-thirty at the bar. You know the same bar we met before."

She remembered, "OK eleven-thirty. I'll be there." They ended the line.

* * *

The club Le Femme was partly crowded, it was eleven o'clock, and from a distance, it looked like the conversation that they were having was secretive, and they appeared to not agree on what they talked about. The dancers were nude as they fondled one another. The fog smoke from the stage spilled over. The lights flashed with different colors, and the music blared loud enough to drown people's conversations into secrecy. In a corner booth, a waitress walked over with their third round of drinks. She placed them down and expected her tip. She was topless, a heavy set rack that looked fake, but perfect. Kalargo gave her a two-dollar tip so she could leave.

"No! You mean to tell me that," He raised his shoulders and opened his eyes to amazement. "You... out of all people can't find someone to go over and do this?" He pushed his diet coke away from him. He sighed and took notice of the dancers.

"Listen, it's not that I or we can't find someone else. The matter is." He took a drink from his gin and orange juice. "We want or prefer someone whom we can trust."

He sat back with his drink in his hand, "Mugumbi, what about him?"

"Too old, we need someone young, which can easily fit into the population. I mean, you are exactly what we need."

He sipped from the glass of diet coke, "You know… this is worse than Jakarta. This is insane." He leaned back and rested his head, let out a huge sigh. He rubbed his face with his left hand vigorously. "How long is this supposed to take?" Kalargo looked at him.

"No more than two weeks, you'll be in and out." Na Min told him.

He smiled and laughed at an inside joke, "That sounds like what I told Jamie when I first met her." They both grinned.

He threw up his hands, "What am I going to tell Jamie? Oh my God, you know this is not something I was expecting to hear. Jamie is going to flip. How am I supposed to get in The Gambia?" before he could say another word. "This sounds like a bad idea to me."

Na Min slammed the rest of his drink down his throat and flagged for the waitress. "Well…" He raised his palms to try to calm him down. "First of all, you will have to fly down to the Philippines for training. That will be at least a week, or two." He hoped he was not counting the weeks as he spoke. "Then we have special transportation that will deliver you to wherever you need to go. From there you will have to parachute into the Gambia under the night sky." Na Min paused.

Kalargo's eyes opened wide, "Parachute?"

"Hold on, you will have everything you would need." He was interrupted.

"Will there be helpers that I can meet with while I am there?"

He looked him in his eyes, "Unfortunately, once you are there. You will be completely on your own." The waitress delivered more drinks.

"This…" he waited for her to leave. "…thank you, this sounds like a suicide mission. A no return deal." He sucked air through his pearly white teeth.

"Listen, if I thought that this was something you could not do or the slightest chance that you would not return. I would not have brought this to you. You are my son, as a son. I gave you my last name. I raised you as if you were my own. This is coming from my heart. I am not saying that this will be a walk in the park. It won't be. This might be one of the most difficult things you will ever do." He was interrupted.

"How much am I going to be paid?" he sipped on his diet coke.

"Two million."

"Two million!" He looked at him with a surprising facial expression. He sighed and downed his drink. "Make it four million, and I'll go."

Na Min put his Genifer back down on the table. "You have a deal, but before I forget…" He held his right hand up to stop him. "…whatever you do, under no circumstance should you ever speak your native language. Never, never, and again never speak your native tongue."

"Is there a reason why?"

"You have two languages that you were born speaking. One of them is the one that you and Mugumbi speak. And then it is the other one that you hardly ever speak and only because you have no one to speak it with. However if someone speaks to you in this native tongue, you must. I cannot stress this enough. You must act like you have no idea what they are talking about. Do you hear me?" he grabbed his hand and looked him in the eyes.

"OK, I hear you. I have not spoken that tongue since I was a kid." He sighed.

The drum rolled his palms on the table, "So the General it is."

Suddenly Jamie walked over to the table, "Hello Na Min." She gave him a kiss on the cheek.

"He was surprised to see her. "Wow, isn't she beautiful?" He looked at him. "No wonder you were crying earlier." He smiled at them both and looked at his watch.

"Wow, he looks at the time…" He stood from the table and slammed his drink. "…well, it was a pleasure to see you again, Jamie." She stood and gave him a hug. He cleared his throat, "Kalargo…" They hugged like father and son, "…you will be hearing from me very soon." He nodded his head as he walked towards the exit.

* * *

The next morning

Jamie walked out of the room half asleep. "Good morning." She wore a nightgown that barely came to her pubic hair. Her nipples were hard and she sighed because she was horny.

"Good morning," Kalargo replied without taking his eyes off the morning paper. The front page read, "Parking Garage Murder"

She grabbed a plastic cup and poured a glass of orange juice. "You want some?"

"Hmm, what are you having, orange juice?"

"Yes." She said.

"Why not, are you cooking breakfast?" She poured him a glass of orange juice and took it to him. "Well I could but I wanted to get some more sleep." She put the glass on the glass coffee table and headed back to the room. He tilted the paper and watched her ass cheeks bounce as she walked on her toes across the floor.

117

"I can wait until you wake up." He continued to read, looking for an article about Saul Kaapuluu's murder. "Hmmm, nothing." he put the paper down and drank his orange juice. He stood up and paused. He noticed how horrible he felt. This nauseous feeling, headaches, and loose bowels were uncontrollable. He let out a huge sigh and walked into his office. He fed the fish and talked to them. "Hey big fella." he flopped into his corporate office chair and thought about Jamie, the trip to Africa, the circumstances, and the what-if. He wondered how to tell Jamie. He thought it would be easier to some way include her, like having her manage the gym while he was gone. It sounded good. Perhaps watch over the house, check the mail, and make sure the lawn was cut, stuff like that. "Yeah, ok." He turned around in the chair. "And don't forget, feed the fish." He sat there thinking for three hours. He tapped his feet the entire time. But he was convinced, this was something he could do, and get away with it. He cracked his knuckles and the bones in his neck. He leaned forward and twisted his back to crack the bones along his vertebrae. He placed his elbows on his knees and placed his face in his palms.

"Damn it." He grabbed his bottom lip with his upper teeth and slowly let it slide away.

He stood up and walked out of his office. Moments later he slowly crawled into bed. Her warm body was soft and desirable. He kissed her shoulder and she turned around and pulled him closer. They made passionate love and fell asleep in each other's arms.

* * *

"Stop!" she screamed. She was having another bad dream. "Please." she cried. He shook her until she was awake. "Jamie, wake up. You are having a bad dream." She looked around with the sheets close to her face. She grabbed him and held him tightly.

"It's OK. You are safe."

"I keep having this dream of this black man hanging from this tree." She buried her face into the pillow. She wiped her tears, sighed and was happy it was just a dream.

"It just seems so real." She shook her head. "So real, like before, last time I had the same exact dream. This guy was hanging upside down from this huge tree." She swallowed her saliva to continue. She sat up to face him. She looked him in his eyes. "Two men were beating him." Her facial expression was like she was really there. Her eyes widened as she told the dream. She turned around and sat with her legs crossed in the Indian position, "Why do I have these silly dreams?" It was very obvious that she was frustrated. "Pass me..." She pointed at the orange juice.

"Maybe you have seen a movie, perhaps a while ago and somehow you are having these nightmares."

"No..." She shook her head, "...and then it's like I always have this dog that, somehow leads me to where this is happening." She explained.

He smiled, "You know what, not trying to be funny, but maybe you should just kill the dog." He nodded his head and they both laughed it off. He comforted her, kissed her, and made her laugh. He locked his lips with hers. She grabbed his mighty python and directed it into the passage of warmth that would lead to another round of passionate love.

Later that night, the phone rang and he answered it, " Hello."

"Sound like you're sleeping." Na Min said.

"Well..." before he could finish, "...I'm calling to tell that by morning you'll know when you will fly out to the Philippines. But go ahead and get your sleep, I'll let you know if the date is official."

He cleared his throat and said, "Ok." The line ended. He looked over his shoulder and knew he would have to tell Jamie. But he let her sleep for now.

* * *

The next morning

Kalargo's office at the gym was filled with laughter. He told a funny story about Bennett. They held their sides, wiped their eyes of tears. He slammed his fist on his desk, "Stop! Stop!" They begged. Kalargo laughed uncontrollably. His back ached, abdominal were tight. Bennett had not walked in yet. He had the office on their knees begging for him to stop. "Just wait till he gets here, he'll tell you." He wipes his eyes with his shirt. "I swear he will tell you the same story. Trust me, I'm not lying." Two of his workers rolled off the couch, they held their sides and tears.

"No more..." they begged. "...you are killing me!" he choked and tried to catch his breath.

Suddenly, Bennett entered the office, and then there was silence, but he could hear the moans of them trying to hold back their laughter. Their faces were filled with this balloon expression of being under pressure. He looked around the office, and he looked at Kalargo. He shook his head because he couldn't hold water. He knew the joke had to be on him. The office exploded with laughter. "Ahhh..." he pointed at him, "...you were telling them about my fat girlfriend?" He shook his head.

A voice from behind, "It's true!" and curled over to the floor.

"Hey, hey..." He raised his hand to defend himself, "...I can't help that I like big bitches, fat girls, if she's not over two hundred fifty pounds of good loving, she is too small." He tried to explain his desire for big gals.

"Man, one day one of the whales is going to hurt your tall skinny ass!" Steve said.

He shook his head and pointed his finger at him, "This one already did."

They fell out with laughter.

He walked over and put his diet coke on the desk. "Wait. Let me tell you how it really happened." He began to tell his side of the story.

"Oh, shiiit…" Kevin said.

"It'll be my pleasure; God knows what he told you guys." He looked at Kalargo. "One day I was riding, minding my own business, my mind was not thinking about any fat bitches, low and behold, I needed some smokes. So, I pulled into the convenience store, you know the one on Taano ave and Wawa." He took a sip of his diet coke. "Now on my way out, I see a crowd of people looking down the street." He pointed in the direction with his hand. "At first I didn't pay it any mind, but after cranking the car and pulling out of the parking lot." He shook his head in disgust. "I'll be God damn if I didn't see this huge fat bitch, just ah running down the street, right. Now…" His eyes open wide; he used his hands to form the shape of this huge whale, and his hands were not close together either. "She passed me. To this day, I never heard of a…" he was lost for words. "Something as big…I mean elephants don't run this fast." The office begged him to stop.

"Now she already caught my eye with her size, right? But she had the Goddamn nerve to have a hot pink mini skirt on, legs and all that ass…" his lips curled up bent crooked. "…bounced around, shit no lie. I got excited as hell." He jumped up and down as they burst into laughter. His eyes became tearful. "Now this bitch running down the street with a jar of damn pickles!" he shook his head wildly, "and it had no top on it! The juice was going everywhere, all on her face, and her clothes." He started to laugh, "Imagine Carl Lewis running the fifty-yard dash, now put him in a hippo outfit with a jar of pickles underneath his arms." He tried to hold his composure. He leaned forward. "And not one pickle came out that jar, not one!" He held his index finger up, took a deep breath, and continued. "She crossed the street going towards that run-down gas

121

station. Man… she fell down, bruised her knees, and elbows, but she didn't lose a pickle!" He took another sip of his diet coke. He stood there biting his bottom lip. He was really into telling his version of the story.

"I paused for a moment…I said to myself." He held his left hand across his heart and right hand over his mouth. "Look, just look at my bitch run! Go, girl, go! That's my bitch right there…" He pointed at the wall. He was so excited. "Man I got to have her!"

"So she ran into the men's room, it was dirty, nasty, the floor was wet, and the smell was like no other…" before he finished.

Kalargo's cell phone rang; he walked out of the office to avoid loud laughter.

Bennett continued, "…now this bathroom had me holding my breath…" he deepens his voice, "…but I entered anyway!" He crossed his eyes and covered his mouth. "This bathroom had writing on the walls, mirrors, like call Candy for free blow jobs, and Kitty Kat Pat has no pussy lips." His entire body shook like he was disgusted. "But…" he held a hand up and changed his voice to this deep Lion King, "I entered anyway!" he lowered his head like he really meant business.

"So I finally saw her, breathing hard as she sat on the wet floor. God knows what was down there before she got there. I looked at this sexy wounded whale." He raised his eyebrows, "Well, I am the eyes of the beholder. I asked her, What the hell are you doing?!" he held his hands over his mouth as if he was really in the bathroom. He spoke through his mouth due to his thumb and index closing off his nose. "We looked at each other with this frantic look on our faces. Now, she had these beautiful Asian eyes, soft smooth skin, not one pimple, her hair was long and wavy. She had blonde streaks. Now her breast had to be in the triple D's. I saw that she was nervous, but it was a moment of love at first sight. Do you guys believe in love at first sight?"

They grinned, wiped their tears, and held their abdominals.

"She sat there in the corner behind the toilet with her hand in the pickle jar. Her wide back spread out like heavy wings on a fat angel. Her knees were pulled inward touching her chest. I will not..." the following words he stressed. "...I will not." He twisted his neck and pointed his finger. "Tell you how turned on I was when I couldn't see her panties due to all of that fat." He smiled and they laughed.

"I..." he held his right hand up to God. "...I love fat bitches. I am a sucker for them." He paused. "I could not see her panties because her fat was just... everywhere. I just knew that she was for me." He licked his chops. "Guess what she asked me?" he looked around the room.

"What!" Steve boldly asked.

"She bit down on a pickle, and said..." He looked sad when he got to this part of the story. "...did anybody else see me come in here? It's my third strike, I can't get caught."

She had her mouth filled with pickles and talking at the same time. He tossed the empty soda can in the trash like he was talking about the world coming to an end. "Fellas...I have had at least five beautiful slim women in my life." He cleared his chest of phlegm and swallowed. "Now, don't look at me like I'm sick, but there is nothing like licking that sweaty salty taste that only sits between the fat of a big woman." He held his tongue out with his eyes closed like a sick lion that has not eaten in forty-five days. He gave everyone in the office chills and creeps. He made their skin crawl as they fell back with disgusting looks on their faces.

"And you know what? That was five years ago." He pulled out a recent picture of her.

"What!" Steve yelled out.

"No way, can't be her?" Damion said.

For the first time, Bennett looked disgusted, sad; he shook his head, "Yep, that's her."

A voice said, "She is gorgeous. What the hell happened?"

Bennett snatched his photo and shoved it back into his wallet with anger. "What happened? Shit… this bitch started exercising, going on this…" he made this strange facial expression. "Damn diet!" He slammed his fist into his left hand, "Can you believe the audacity, now she wanted to go on a fucken diet." He shook his head.

Steve stood up, "What a damn minute. You are saying that you are pissed that she lost the weight?"

He grunted and sighed, he vigorously rubbed his hands through his hair. "Guys…" he looked like a poor wounded hyena. "…I pray, I pray to five different Gods…" he started counting with his thumb to his pinky finger, "…to please bring my fat bitch back home." The office was filled with laughter.

"No, I am serious, I want me…" He held his hands up in front of him, "…everything about her, the roundness, gone! Big BREAST, GONE! Her ass, GONE! You could just say my dream bitch, GONE!" he tossed his right hand over his shoulder.

"So why haven't you left her yet?" a new guy asked.

"We've been through so much together, most of all, I love her." He walked over to the shelf behind Kalargo's desk and pulled out a magazine. She was on the cover. "I am so proud of her. I…" He was interrupted.

The door opened. "Bennett… I need to talk to you." Kalargo nodded his head to talk with him in private.

* * *

Later that night Kalargo called Jamie.

"Jamie, what are you doing?" She was happy to hear from him.

"I need to talk to you. Are you able to come over?" He could not find an easy way to tell her.

"Of course… you sound a little down. Are you ok?" her voice was concerned.

He pulled the cellular away from his ear and sighed with a frustrated expression. "Oh no I am good, I just wanted to talk to you, spend a little time together. I'll be here when you arrive; just drive on in, the gate will be open."

After she arrived, he told her he was going on a business trip that will last two months. He explained how he wanted her to run the gym while he was gone. He had already told his staff that she would be in charge with the help of one of his employees. He also wanted her to check the mailbox, make sure the landscapers cut the grass, and most importantly to feed the fish. She sat there on the edge of the bed like she had seen a ghost.

"But, when do you have to leave?" she asked with a childish look, reached for his hand, and held it tight. She kissed his hand and rubbed it across her face to wipe her tears.

"In six hours." He rubbed his hands through her hair, Her eyes filled with tears. "You have to… so soon?"She looked in the corner of the room and saw that his carry-on bag was filled, ready, and waiting.

"Oh my God Kalargo, I did not know you would have to go so soon." She stood up on her tiptoes and locked her lips on his like a kissing fish. He slowly.moved his lips to her eyebrows. He held her face in his palms and placed his forehead on hers, "I will miss you."

"Are you going to call me?" she asked.

"Of course, I will, every chance I get, I will call you…" he whispered to her ear.

"So that means I can call you?" she waited for him to say yes.

"Yes…" He wrapped his arms around her and locked his fingers. "…I will have a global phone with me." He sighed. Their French kiss followed with a round of passionate love.

Chapter Eleven

Seoul, South Korea

Na Min sat at the dinner table resting his left elbow and holding his reading glasses to his mouth. His wife cooked and prepared their food. The house smelled like rice and chicken, the Puerto Rican dish that they loved. He had returned from Hawaii the day before and the pressure from the North Koreans to send Kalargo to kill the General, weighed heavy on his mind. He knew that he was more than capable of this mission, but anything can happen and that's what concerned him. He also thought about the damage he has done over the years by giving the North Koreans Top Secret information, it looked like his retirement was his only way out.

He never thought he would ever betray his country, but greed took him under at a time when he was vulnerable, weak, and hurt. In Thailand, he saw how fellow servicemen smuggled heroin on military planes, not I, he had told himself. But this was no different, he felt. Maybe if he had said something, perhaps all of this could have turned out differently. He shook his head and thought if he had a chance to do it all over again. He would do it all differently. All the money in the world could not replace the pride he had. He rubbed his right hand across his heart. He remembered when he used to pledge allegiance when he was in high school in Seattle, Washington. Now his heart felt like an over-matured rotten mango that had been stepped on and remained beneath someone's shoe.

His plate was placed in front of him, cranberry juice to the left. She returned with her food and sat down. She grabbed his hand and they closed their eyes to pray. He had to ask God to forgive him. He could hear his wife's voice as she prayed out loud, beneath his breath he thanked him for every day he had breathed and forgive him for taking the breath of others. He slowly opened his eyes and realized that she was waiting on him to open his.

"Are you ok?" she sipped her cranberry juice.

He drove the fork into the yellow rice, "Yeah, of course, este es bien." He closed his eyes and chewed on his food.

"Oh, you are practicing your Spanish?" They laughed, held hands and kissed.

"One of these months we should fly over to Puerto Rico." He said.

She looked at him and smiled. "Now that sounds like a good idea."

"How is the weather in two months?" he asked her.

"Are you serious?" she was happy. "It's gorgeous…" she tried to continue.

"Now don't quote me, it's just a thought." He put another fork full in his mouth and they enjoyed their dinner as they talked about the Caribbean Islands.

Later that night they cuddle in bed and watched American TV. He slowly closed his eyes and daydreamed.

It was 1979 Osan, South Korea, in the middle of winter. The door opened and the sound of the blistering wind that blew snowflakes behind Agent Bradley was silenced when the door slammed shut. He stomped his feet and brushed off the snowflakes that covered his walnut mink trench coat. He snatched off his gloves and looked Na Min dead in his eyes. The sound of the burning wood in the fireplace, the smell of it lingered the safe house that was fifteen miles outside the city, and three hours from North Korea.

Na Min sat at the dinner table lighting his tobacco pipe. He wore a caramel thick wool turtle neck sweater, a pair of blue jeans with three pairs of long johns beneath them. His beard was six months of not shaving.

"I thought we were partners?" Bradley threw his gloves on the table and walked over to him in a disturbing manner. He planted the palm of his hands on the dinner table.

Na Min expressed no emotions, and took a drag from his cigar and allowed his smoke to rise in his face. "What are you talking about?" Na Min looked at him.

"Na Min, what's going on man? We have known each other for a long time, and I know when things are not right." Bradley said.

He stood up from the table and grabbed his coat, gloves, and hat that covered his ears. "I told you last week that the drop spot had changed. Did you follow the signs?" Na Min said.

"What signs? You did not tell me about any signs!" Bradley looked confused.

Na Min sighed and knew it was time to get this over with. His pain of broken trust was up to his throat. No matter how he tried to forgive and forget, his voice had begun to gnaw at him like maggots. He kept his furious temper in control. "Let's go, grabbed your belongings, I guess I have to show you these signs in person." Na Min exhaled his smoke through his nostrils like a mad bull.

They left the house and drove forty-five minutes north of the safe house. The weather had worsened; the ground was covered with four feet of snow. The heat in the car was on full blast.

"No wonder you can't see the signs, they are covered by the snow." The chit-chat continued, "You make a left turn here." He parked the car and they both got out. There was an old farmhouse that had not been lived in for five years or more. They walked behind the barn to search for documents. Bradley stopped; he saw a hole that was six feet deep with a small amount of snow in it. He turned around and Na Min had his .45 caliber in his face.

"What the hell are you doing? Are you crazy?" The look on his face was of shock.

Na Min waved the gun at him. "I trusted you." He looked at him. He just had to say these final words. He sighed deeply. "I've been trying to hold this deep anger in for too long."

"But..." Bradley tried to speak.

"Shut up! I don't want to hear it. You destroyed everything I had planned. I was happy. You took away the one thing that I had pride in. Do you know how important family is?" He backed away from him. The wind had reduced their body temperatures. Their faces and toes were going numb, and the feeling of being in the middle of nowhere worried him. He let out visible thick breath from his nose and mouth.

"Na Min..." He held up his hands, and swallowed his saliva, "...relax ok, we can talk this out. We... don't have to do this." He begged him.

He raised his voice, "You think I did not know!?" He gritted his teeth with frustration. He tried to walk away from the grave. The sound of the gun went off. "Don't move! Do you really think I don't know? Who do you think requested for you to get transferred for duty? Me! I wanted you here. I wanted you! I have tried to get you here for six months. You were denied duty in South America because of me!" he talked and Bradley looked down at the grave.

"Listen, what are you talking about? Are you losing your mind?" The gun went off again, he fell. "Ouch, ahh…" he grabbed his left leg and screamed, "…ass hole…" He shot him again, in the other leg.

"You still want to pretend you don't know what this is about! She told me everything. Na Min tears fell from his eyes. He had been hurting for so long. He had asked God to forgive him for sleeping with his wife Kandace. He had forgiven his wife but just could not forgive him. Deep down inside, torn apart; his anger of the thoughts was eating him alive.

With the sound of his cries, he begged for his life. "Na Min, please. Don't do it."

He put the gun to his own head, but he could not do it. "Why…" Na Min asked.

"You were never home. She needed someone to be there." He applied pressure to his wounds, "Get me to a hospital, I am going to die out here."

"Die piss ant. I want you to feel what I have been feeling. I have been holding this shit in for way too long. You will die… slow!"

"You want to know something that has been, well a little TOP SECRET mother fucker?" He cracked a smile, a sarcastic one that did not last long. "Justin was your…" he pointed the pistol at him. "…son, that's correct ass hole." He was starting to feel the chill of winter crawl down his back, numb his ears, and fingers.

Bradley looked at him and before he pulled the trigger he asked him for one favor. He begged him to listen. "What about my daughter? Can you look out for Yuki?" he wanted to be told that he would look out for her. He wanted to hear it from his mouth. "And let her know that her father loved her."

Before he squeezed the trigger, "I'll grant you that. I will take her in as my own and I'll always let her know that you loved her." The three gunshots silenced the farm, the cries, the anger, and the hate.

Na Min opened his eyes and looked at his wife. She was sound asleep. He crawled out of bed in need of a sleeping pill that had been prescribed to him. He shook his head and swallowed them and fell asleep.

* * *

Philippine training camp

The heat and humidity were like wearing a plastic bag with a hundred insects crawling over him. Kalargo was exhausted, sleepy, hungry, and thirsty. The jungle training was intense. He crawled through the muddy wet rain forest where everything imaginable lived. He had crawled for three miles, swim across rivers, swamps, peeled leeches from his back, neck, and stomach like relentless duck tape. He carried a small container of water that he could drink every five hours. He was on very strict water consumption for the entire thirty days he had been there. His urine had to be as pure as possible. This was a three-day exercise that required him to survive off of the jungle. He didn't mind the taste of snakes, frogs, and grasshoppers. They were everywhere and easy to catch, and cook. The grasshoppers were a lot easier to catch and swallow so he would grab them as he made his way through the dense jungle.

He looked up at the night sky and saw how beautiful it was. The stars were so bright. It was his final night of training and he was so close to finishing in record time. So he pushed on to the finish. He came from a grassy area onto a road that led him to a waiting jeep. The early morning sun crawled out like it was tired of rising. The fellow waiting for him was sound asleep.

"Good morning," Kalargo said.

The Pilipino rebel was startled that he had arrived so soon. He looked at the stopwatch and pushed the button. He spoke in his dialect and tried to speak English but manage to communicate. "You are passed." He said with a smile that had missing, rotten, decayed teeth.

"It's fast, with an f. Fast." He tried to correct him. In the Philippine dialects, they pronounce their p's like f's and their f's like p's.

"I am starving." he rubbed his stomach to show him what he was saying.

"Yes." he pointed. "Let go." He cranked the jeep and drove off into the sunrise. He tried talking to the driver, but his English was so horrible. It was like trying to talk to six monkeys that studied the Rosetta Stone course. So he gave up the conversation and let the driver talk to himself. He inhaled the armpit of his shirt and frowned, in need of a shower, and a good night's sleep.

After breakfast, he did his final urine test. He was pissing water by now. He held it up, "Now that is clean." He smiled and handed it to the doctor, Now I can have a diet coke?" He asked the doctor.

The short Pilipino doctor tightens the lid on the cap and said, "No your urine has to maintain clarity for drinking, you can't drink the water there. You will have to drink your own urine if clean water is not available." He turned around and gave him a plastic bag. "These are your furipiers." They looked like small tubular sugar packages. He opened the plastic bag to notice the different flavors. "These are to kill the taste in your urine. These..." He pulled one from the bag to show him. "...I recommend that you start with the lemon flavor first." The doctor said.

Kalargo stood up and walked towards the door. "Doctor... I don't think I could actually drink my own urine." He looked at him.

The doctor smiled, "What do you mean? Your urine has been clean for the last fifteen days, what do you think you have been drinking from your canteen? The only difference, the water in your canteen was half and half water, unflavored." He looked him in his eyes like it was no surprise. He pushed up his shoulders like. "I thought you knew already."

Kalargo's jaw dropped and he sighed. "No way..."

"No one told you? Well hey now you know, but make sure..." He held his right index finger up. "...do not lose these. Keep them in this plastic bag. Believe me, you will use them sooner or later."

He walked out of the makeshift medical office and sighed as he looked up at the sky. A voice came from behind him, "Kalargo... we finally meet." Zang spoke in Korean.

"And who are you?" he asked him in Korean.

He bowed and he did the same. "I am Zang. I came a long way to meet you." They shook hands. "I wanted to personally meet you." He directed him to his waiting car. He opened the back door for him and they both chatted as the driver drove around the small terrorist camp.

He had noticed Zang's throat had been slashed and the left side of his face had third-degree burns from years ago. His hair did a poor job of covering his ear which was reduced to a hole on the side of his head. His voice was hard to understand due to his throat being damaged. That made his Korean harder to comprehend. "I have to apologize for my Korean. I am lacking the practice. Do you speak English?"

Zang laughed as his skin tighten. He blushed.

He tried not to stare at his wounds and that hole on the side of his head.

"Kalrago..." He looked at him. "I speak perfect English." He laughed. "So... in the morning you will be flying out at four am." He reached in his coat pocket and gave him all the documents that he would need. "Airline tickets, a new passport from Canada...driver can you lower the air condition?"

"Yes, Mr. Zang." The driver replied.

"When you arrive in Afghanistan, you will change planes to a non-commercial plane to a humanitarian flight to a country in Africa and then you parachute into the Gambia. All of your equipment will be parachuted along with you. Do you have any questions?"

He held the documents in his hand. He read the name on the Canadian driver's license. He sighed. He noticed that the airline tickets were purchased through WORLDBRIDGETAVEL.COM.

"Well, I guess I don't have any questions. Phone... Can I use your phone?" Kalargo asked.

Zang hesitated. "Well due to security reasons..." He sighed.

"I understand. Everything is a security reason." Kalargo tapped the documents on his thigh. Moments later they pulled up in front of his living quarters.

"Kalargo, I want to wish you good luck and a safe return." They shook hands and he exited the car.

* * *

The Gambia, Africa

General Kakambo Twigani stood 5'8, a hundred eighty pounds, dark complexion, and short Afro. His hair looked pushed back like an unwanted hat. At the age of forty-two, he became the General of the Gambian Army while his older brother sat on the throne as King.

Their family has ruled the Gambia for more than eighty years. The General smoked Cuban cigars back to back. He always released his smoke through his wide nose like a bull, wore pressed olive green camouflage, and maintained spit-shined boots. He had lost a lot of soldiers and desperately wanted to know who was behind the supply of the enemy troops. He gave orders to kill any rebel fighter, and take no prisoners. The Gambia was in chaos. He chopped a father's head off because his son did not know his name. He felt that if his son did not know who he was. His father had to be a rebel.

"General!" an officer entered his office standing at attention with good news to report. He saluted the General. After returning his salute, he approached his desk.

The General converted an abandoned church that was riddled with bullet holes into his headquarters. His office was located in the basement. The paint on the walls had peeled and distorted the faces of the painted angels. His photo of him in his younger days hung behind him. The dust blanked the cracked concrete floor; Cuban cigar smoke lingered and found its way out every time the door opened.

"We have gained control of the cities of Kaba, Gubio, and Mostiwa." the officer said. The entire church vibrated after a bomb exploded, dust floated from the ceiling.

General Twigani removed his cigar from his mouth with his right hand. He stood with excitement. "Yes!" He walked around the small four-legged table and stood in front of the map that hung on the wall. He exhaled smoke from his nose and pointed to the map with his cigar between his fingers. "We have to have this town back." He said with his back facing the officer. He spoke about his hometown.

"What town is that?" the officer walked over and stood next to him.

"The town of Diabugu." He took a long drag as the cherry brighten on the cigar.

Officer Baggihk closed his eyes as the smoke irritated them.

"How's your family doing?" The General asked him.

"Sir it's war, they are either dead or relocated to refugee camps."

The General turned around and looked up at the ceiling. "I would consider yourself lucky. The King and I are the only survivors in our family. For our family's sake, we must win this war. Don't you agree?" He looked at him. He placed red flag thumbtacks on the cities of Wassu, Kunting, and Bansang.

"Of course."

Dust floated from the ceiling again. "How hard can it be to find the bastards that are bombing the runway?" before the officer could respond.

"Yes, we have control of the airport, but what good is it if we can't land on the damn thing." His cigar was short and midget-like compared to a new one. "I have a question for you, do you know who is supplying these rebels?" the General walked over to his desk and put the cigar out in the ashtray.

"You will be the first to know." He said.

"Coffee?" He offered the officer as he poured his own.

"No, sir. I have work to do. Thanks anyway." He saluted the General, "Permission to leave sir?"

The General returned his salute and the officer walked out of the office, dust floated from the ceiling, he looked up and sighed.

Chapter Twelve

Seoul, South Korea

Yuki lay next to Mugumbi with tears slowly falling sideways towards her ear. His right leg crossed her legs as he lay asleep. They both snuggle under a purple silk comforter that had small designs of gold umbrellas. She opened her blurry wet eyes to see the white carpeted bedroom. She saw herself in the mirrored wall across from the bed. The sound of the water bed occasionally rippled. She turned over to her left side and looked at the clock. She closed her eyes and tried not to think of her biological father, CIA agent Bradley.

Yuki's mother died when she was born. Her father was the best thing she ever had. She frequently dreamed of her father's funeral, and how Na Min walked her up to his casket. He held her hand and picked her up as they got closer. She slowly fell back to sleep under Mugumbi's arms.

* * *

The smell of blueberry candles danced in Na Min's newly decorated office. The leather cream sofa against the far wall with an oil-based painting of him. He sat there with a picture in his left hand of his family, wife, and children. He removed his reading glasses to wipe a falling tear. Beneath his eyes were puffy and his face had grown wrinkle over the years. He rubbed his forehead with his right hand. He had a receding hairline with a substantial amount of gray hair. But for an old man, he was in good health.

He went into deep thought that took him back thirty years. He was twenty-five years old on his first assignment for the CIA in Central America. As an Intelligence officer, it was his duty to train the rebels and interrogate prisoners; all information was directly reported to his senior officer in D.C.

San Salvador was a beautiful country with some of the most gorgeous people in the region. However, it was also a place of many horrors, and these horrors eventually consumed him. Na Min had become a vicious cold-blooded killer, bloodthirsty was a better way of describing him. His methods of interrogating went from the norm to the extreme, even torture, and death. He had grown accustomed to witnessing and participating in some of the most horrific tortures to mankind. He was highly recommended for leading all interrogations. He no longer followed the rules of Geneva. He was known to be out of control.

The morning of June 8, four am, he crawled and inched his way between two bushes, with his binoculars to his eyes, the muddy dirt painted his face. He focused on a communist rebel army camp. "Let me see what we have here." He whispered out to a San Salvadorian platoon leader.

"Now, if I could find out who is supplying them their weapons?" He sighed and passed the binoculars to the platoon leader. "Look, tell me what you see just passed the tent."

Na Min rolled over to his left. He wore green fatigues and black soldier boots. His uniform had no insignia or country of origin. It took ten days of crossing the jungle. The platoon of novice soldiers was exhausted but under good leadership.

The small camp consisted of approximately forty rebels and lots of supplies. It was imperative that he find out the supply route and supplier. "Juan, in that tent I believe there are at least twelve soldiers." he reached for the binoculars with his left hand. He slowly pulls a leaf down to get a better view. "In one hour, we will be able to see better with the early morning sunrise." He whispered.

"Na Min, I think it would be better if we call in for an airstrike," Juan said.

Na Min sighed, "Just make sure we don't blow everything to pieces, I would like to be able to interrogate someone this time."

"Hey don't blame that last one on me. I had a new radioman. He gave the coordinates." Juan explained.

"Well either the radioman could not read your writing or you gave him the wrong coordinates. Either way, we can't afford to not get a lead on this supply trail. I mean just imagine how far we have come. If we blow this, I can truly say your country will be in a civil war for many years to come." he looked at him and patted him on the shoulder. "It would be big news if the Russians are supplying but even worse, Fidel," Na Min said and slapped the back of his neck to kill a mosquito. "It's all the same, If the Cubans or the Russians. Everybody knows who backed Cuba, but to have someone to point the finger would make it a lot easier." Na Min said.

Juan approached three of his soldiers, "Listen, in one hour, take seven men and set up a perimeter on the left flank." He said as he reached deep into his shirt to pull out a map.

"Gomez, take six of your guys just on the right flank." He pulled his flashlight out and held it between his teeth to keep a steady aim on the map. He closely examined the map to coordinate the airstrike. "Now Gomez, take these, you see the tent right there?"

"Si senor." he peered through the binoculars, "Na Min believes the most important people in the camp are there, so you know what that means?"

Gomez used his arm sleeve to wipe the sweat from his forehead and nose. "Si yo se que debo de hacer." He tried to speak his English, "Shoot for legs, no-kill." He pointed at Carlos's legs.

Na Min sat beneath a tree thinking his plan through. He hoped to have at least five prisoners to interrogate. Juan came from behind; "Smokes?" he pulled one from the pack and Juan lit them both.

"In fifteen minutes…" He looked at his watch and let out a huge puff of smoke. "Gomez and Jose will have their teams in

position."

After the airstrike, the smell of burning flesh, rubber, and debris filled the air. The injured can be heard, but slowly and quietly dying off. His special team of four waited for the green light that everything was secured. The crackling sound that came over the radio said, "Todo bien, todo bien, operacion exito."

"OK boys and girls let's see what we have here to work with." Na Min said to his team.

They used their machetes to cut through the three hundred feet of dense jungle and down the slope that led them to the camp. He patiently walked through the camp using his feet and occasionally his hands to turn bodies over. "Hmmm…" he mumbled with the tip of the cigarette but barely hanging between his lips. Juan came over with excitement, jumping over debris and bodies.

"Senor, we have fifteen prisoners for interrogation." He sighed and wiped his sweat from his forehead. His armpits were wet and his American m-16 was strapped around his back.

"Well, let's get this party started." he said with confidence, "If anyone knows anything, we'll get it out of them." He took a deep drag from his cigarette. "Juan, set up a makeshift tent here and I want you to put the prisoners…" he pointed. "… there."

He immediately started snapping his fingers and yelling in Spanish. "Na Min, one of my soldiers found some documents-you might be interested in." He told him as he pulled out his box of cigarettes from his top left pocket.

The young soldier gave the documents to him. He looked no older than sixteen years old. He looked over the papers. "Now this…" he waved the papers above his right shoulder. "…is interesting." He stuffed the papers in his right side pants pocket. "Where are these so-called prisoners?"

They brought fifteen guys, some were tied, and others too wounded to tie up. They all looked like they wished they were dead. Na Min slowly walked through them, looking at each one. He finally made his decision. "Him!" he pointed.

Their eyes opened wide and the fear on his face closed his mouth with a wrinkle pout. A soldier picked him up by the back of his shirt collar and practically dragged him to the front of the group.

"Juan, I want you to translate for me. Tell the rest of them that I am here for information only. They can make it easy or hard. I have all day, but I won't spend all day asking the same questions. I personally don't..." He kind of waved his hands in the air with a sarcastic grin, "...have that kind of all-day patients. However, there will be an award for cooperating."

Juan could be heard translating every word like a bilingual parrot. He continued, and the prisoners paid close attention as Na Min walked towards his first prisoner. He used his right thumb to close off his right nostril, blew mucous from his nose, and wiped his hand on the back of his pants.

"Are you a talker?" He waited for a response, "Tommy, bring me that can of gas."

He was cold-hearted, by now he had over forty-two murders under his belt. In a normal world he would be considered a serial killer, but in this situation, location, circumstances, he is the God of information extraction, but an example always had to be set, and unfortunately. Any many miny moe, either way, somebody will have to die first.

The soldier started speaking Spanish. As far as he was concerned, he had no real use for him. He knew this poor peasant was worthless. He had chosen him just to kill. He was no more than an insect to him, someone to torture to get the others ready to talk. He knew they'd be begging to talk first.

He looked in the eyes of the others and saw the fear in their eyes, but it was the same fear that he had seen before, not fearful enough. Some mumbled Spanish reiterate of some sort, others began crying with those senseless crocodiles tears that won't save them. The sound of the match grew the cries wider. Their death was imminent at the hands of a monster. Some looked up like they had an unforgiving God.

"Na Min, I think we can interrogate a different way! This is insane!" Juan spoke out loud.

"You think so!" as a monster on steroids; "I don't have any more patients to dick around with these dirt farmers!" he walked over to him.

142

He put the match to his cigarette and inhaled. He looked at him directly in his eyes. "These are the same farmers who are resisting and fighting against democracy." With a calm and mellow voice, Na Min blows smoke over his shoulder. He takes a visual survey of Juan's soldiers watching the scene. He leaned in closer and whispered in his left ear, "Juan don't ever interrupt my God damn interrogation, ever, under any circumstances, claro?" He patted him on the shoulder and smiled at everyone else.

"Si Senor." Juan felt threatened.

Na Min turned around and slowly walked over to the prisoner that was soaked in gasoline. "Juan! Tell these bastards they have two minutes to tell me where and who is supplying them ammo, weapons, and bla bla bla" He pointed his index finger at each of them, with his right boot he pushed a small pile of dirt back and forward.

The early morning sun gave light to the damage to the camp. Most of his soldiers were gathering what they could. His team surrounded the prisoners with additional soldiers from the platoon watching. "Translate, if you dirt farmers want to save this poor comrade of yours from burning a painful death..." he inhaled on his cigarette. Juan's voice can be heard translating in the background. Three of the prisoners started saying, "Padre Nuestro que esta en el cielo, santificado sea tu nombre..." Those that did not have a higher power chose other final words to comfort them. "Speak your mind to forever hold your peace." he put the cigarette close to the wet prisoner. The prisoner closed his eyes and screamed, quickly saying the Lord's Prayer, "Padre Nuestro, que esta en el cielo, santificado sea tu nombre..."

Just before he flicked the cigarette, a brave soul yelled out, "Te hablare!"

Na Min quickly pointed him out as God gave him this power to torture human beings. "Take him! Translate! If you lie to me, any of you, I will know!"

The prisoner was dragged across the early morning dark wet dirt with his hands tied in front of him. He begged to spare his life.

"Ask him! Where and who is supplying them?" His voice echoed throughout the camp.

The nearby birds flew away to safety. With the sound of a grown man crying, the prisoner was covered in blood and dirt. He looked malnourished and pitiful. He bowed back and forward, begging and pleading for forgiveness in Spanish.

Juan translated, "He said, 'Please don't kill his brother. He is the last brother that he has." He paused to see how he would respond.

"What does he know about the supplies?!" Na Min demanded.

The prisoner's hands were up to his face begging him like a helpless peon. He crawled towards Carlos. He held onto his left leg like a child that is happy to see their father. Carlos kicked him in the face. He proceeded towards Na Min like an animal begging for food. He praised and kissed his boots. He snatched his left foot and then his right boot away from his lips. "This is pathetic and depressing. What is he saying? Did he answer my question?"

Juan sighed heavily, with his mouth filled with air. He slowly let it out and shook his head. His five o'clock shadow beard gave him this exhausted look on his face. He didn't want to tell him what he had said.

"What did he say?!" Na Min asked.

"He said he does not know anything about where and how…" He combs his right hand through his hair, "…he is begging you not to kill his brother. They are the last men in their family." He looked up at the sky and rubbed his five o'clock shadow beard.

"Well, I can see for myself that he is begging Juan!" Na Min paused. "So nobody knows anything." He walked around the prisoners to come in between the brothers. "I am not here for family counseling, family matters, or any other crap they will try to throw at me. I want facts, info, and what the hell are two brothers doing the fighting." He pointed his finger at them both.

"You knew you two were not going to make it…" He cracked an ugly smile at them. He sighed and cleared his throat and tried to spit but it hung from his mouth like a long spaghetti noodle that would not break away. He used his left hand to break it off. "Juan, tell him for his brother's sake… I won't kill his only brother…" he played with a small pile of dirt with his left boot.

The prisoner became joyful. He crawled over to his brother and put his tied hands around him and cried. Na Min walked over to them both and pulled out his .45 caliber and shot him. "But, I did not say I would spare you." He said as he stood over them both. The smoke lingered from the barrel. One shot to the chest, and he watched him struggle for his final breath for four minutes. The brother screamed as his older brother bled to death with his arms around him.

The silence among the prisoners was like they had died, speechless, the fear kept them quiet. Suddenly, three soldiers tried to get away. "Shoot them in the legs! Now I have who I am looking for." He smiled and put his .45 in his holster and fastened the leather strap.

"I want these three separated from each other. Have the rest start digging holes. If they are too injured to dig, kill them!" he yelled out loud, "It was about time we got down to the bottom of this mess. After they dig the holes…" He whispered to Carlos. "… Kill them all."

* * *

Six months later

Washington D.C.

"Today is promotion day." Na Min embraced his wife and locked his lips
with hers. He rubbed her back and soothed her muscles.

"I am so glad you invited the family to join you. You have no idea
how much we have missed you." She told him with her Eskimo kisses.
Kandace remained a stunning blonde for having two kids. She stood 5'9
at a hundred twenty-five pounds. She was not bad for an ex-model. She
thought about going back into the modeling business just to keep her
busy. She ran five miles a day and dieted to remain in shape. They met in
college in a fitness gym. She was attracted to Asian men as he was
attracted to blondes. She set aside her career goals to be with him. She
wore a white blouse and blue jean shorts, her hair pinned up in a bun.
She walked across the hotel room, stepped over Cynthia, and called for
Justin. "Are you hiding again?" She asked with a smile as she entered the
bathroom. From the bathroom her voice can be heard "Honey, maybe we
could do this more often..." she looked out from the bathroom door, so
happy to be with him. "...you know, travel and meeting you in different
locations. That would be nice, right?" She ducked back into the
bathroom, grabbed her toothbrush and toothpaste. She walked out with
the toothbrush in her mouth.

Na Min knew that would be a security risk. Before he could
disappoint her, she said "I know everyone has a job to do..." she stood in
front of him, cheerful, and talking with a mouth full of toothpaste,
smoothly brushing her teeth. "But I know the agency, perhaps that would
be a risk of security, right?" she asked.

He stood up, "Damn, you are right, but if I could get around it, you
bet we all would be in some of the places that I go to."

She returned to rinse her mouth, "And then we could visit all the beautiful cities that you go to."

"Daddy, what time are we leaving?" Cynthia asked. She had been asking to go to the Washington D.C. Zoo every since she saw the hotel pamphlet.

Justin, her younger brother came from under the bed. "Yeah, don't forget parrot jungle."

Cynthia pinched him and said, "Parrot Jungle is in Florida."

Justin rubbed his arm with a frown and began to cry. She walked over to apologize, but he balled into a fetal position and hid beneath the bed.

"Justin boy, stop crying and be a big boy." Na Min changed his voice to soothe his pain, "Stop letting these girls see you cry." He stood in front of the bed and picked him up, tickled him until he heard him laugh. "You aren't hurt, boy stop playing."

His head peeked through with a big smile. "I love you, daddy."

"I love you too." He held him high and bounced him onto the bed.

Then Cynthia jumped on the bed. "Look mommy look."

Kandace smiled, looked at the hotel clock. "OK kids, it's time to go to bed. We have an early wake-up call." The laughter that smeared the room settled down.

"Did you put in for the 7 o'clock wakeup call?" Na Min asked.

"No, actually 8 am, did you want 7 am?" she looked at him.

"Hmmm, 8 am is good, ok kids settle down and get ready for bed." He said.

The hotel phone rang. "Yes hello, this is Marriott guest services. We are confirming your wake-up call for 8 am correct?" before she could respond, "We also would like to offer a full breakfast delivered to your room, free of charge, are you interested?"

"One moment please." She put them on hold.

"Yes, we would be interested."

"What time would you want breakfast to be delivered?"

"9 am sharp." She looked at him, he didn't disagree.

"It will be the continental breakfast for a party of four; it comes with a jug of orange juice, milk, and croissants."

"Thank you." Moments later she softly placed the receiver on the phone.

Na Min tossed and turned throughout the night. His sleeping medication kept the nightmares to a minimum. He finally opened his eyes to look at the clock.

"Damn..." he sighed, "...still too early." He rubbed his eyes and cleared his throat. The clock said four thirty am. He twisted his back until his bones cracked one after another. He twisted his head to his left and right to crack his neck bones. He stood up and bent down to touch his toes, and forced his forehead to touch his knees. The room was dark with only the television on. The broadcast had ended and the sound of static echoed the family suite. He paused and looked at how uncomfortable his son looked as he lay on the bed. He walked over and tucked him neatly, kissed him on the forehead, and thought of all the freedom that they have. He walked over to the window and pulled the curtain to look from the sixth floor. An inch of snow had fallen overnight, and the remaining flurries floated softly. In the distance, he could see the white house and Capitol Hill. He closed the curtain and walked into the bathroom and pissed. The sound of falling liquid echoed until it dripped. He grabbed a small amount of tissue to wipe the toilet seat and flushed. He looked into the mirror as he washed his hands. He looked at his tattoo of a lion head with a torn arm in his mouth. He rubbed it and thought of the day he had it done. He quickly hit the light switch, it brought back so many memories.

He crawled back into bed and held his wife tight, "Honey…" She spoke in a low voice and turned on to her right side. She felt his breath on the back of her neck. His lips nibbled her ear. Her left hand reached behind her buttocks to caress his mighty python. She stroked him until his erection was powerful. His left hand found its way between her legs. Her breathing became heavy as his middle finger groped her lips, pushed her clit to the left, right, and finally snorkeled its way deep into her wet pawn. She held him as his breathing increased with his heartbeat. Suddenly, they stopped and looked across the room.

"They still sleep?" she asked.

"Hmm, yeah." he moved his middle finger faster. She put her left hand to her mouth and licked her palm twice to lubricate her palm.

"Oh my," he said. He penetrated deep and she stroked him faster. He stopped to look at the children. "Still sleep?"

She squeezed his monster tight, gritted her teeth, and threatened him with a horny agitated whispering voice, "If you stop again when I'm ready to cum. I will snatch it off!"

He quickly rotated his index finger across her clit, her back arched. She grabbed the sheets into a bundle. He spoke softly in her ear. "Let's finish this in the bathroom."

She stopped and looked at the kids. They were sound asleep. With a smile, she French kissed him and tossed the bedsheets to the floor. He held his head back and slowly caressed her head. They made passionate love until they could no longer stand. The print of her back smeared the mirror. Their bodies were weak and sweaty. He placed her on the edge of

149

the sink and vacuumed her love pawn dry; her knees trembled as she moaned beneath her breath.

"Quack Quack!" he stepped on a rubber duck as he picked her up and carried her to the bedroom. She held him tight with her arms around his neck; she licked his sweat from his face and shoved her tongue down his throat. He placed her on the bed and lay next to her naked underneath the sheets. Their heartbeats slowly came to a normal strong thump. Their overworked bodies felt heavy, it didn't take them long to fall asleep.

The sunrise eased its way between the curtains and the early wakeup call tortured them. "My God, please answer that." She picked up the receiver and placed it back down. "Honey, it's time to get up." She said with her thumb and index finger closing his nose. His eyes opened with a moan and turned over. His right leg hung off the edge of the bed. His right arm lay beneath his body. She embraced him. "I love you." She said.

He moaned, lifted his head, and looked over at the kids. His head fell like a bowling ball into the pillow. "Yeah yeah..." he said in Korean.

Kandace lay across from him. She looked at the kids and turned to him. "Are you ready for round two?"

"Hell no." He mumbled in Korean.

"Oh, what does that mean?" She smiled with her right hand beneath the sheets and held his Johnson. "Looks like somebody is ready for round two." She smiled.

"Well in Korean, that means hell, no, but you can run my shower for me." He smiled.

She smiled, licked her beautiful lips, and tossed her hair from her face, "Anything for my Emperor."

He watched her sexy ass walk across the room; he smiled and knew that he was the luckiest man alive.

She wakes the kids as he showered; his 1:30 pm meeting with the director of the CIA will be in Langley, Virginia. He had murdered a lot of people to get this information and it has finally paid off. He discovered the North Koreans were supplying the rebels; he had photos, and documents to prove it.

"Honey, did you pack my republican tie... you know my favorite red tie with the gold leaves on it?" he asked while he was drying off. He could hear her mumbling, it took her a moment to search the luggage. She sighed in disappointment and knew this was his favorite tie that his father gave him. He always felt like it was his good luck charm. It made him feel confident and gave him a sense of empowerment.

"Damn, how could I have forgotten it?" She questioned herself, "Honey." She spoke sadly. It didn't sound like she had found it. "I completely forgot it. I swear I took it out of the closet..." She tries to explain before he gets upset. She remembered how he responded the last time he got upset over wasted toothpaste a while back. She stopped and said no more. It was silent for a moment, she thought quickly, "Hey I'll run down and get another tie."

He walked out of the bathroom, "Don't worry about it. You go ahead get the kids ready and I'll run down to the gift shop to get something." He held the towel around his neck and put his lips on hers. She smiled and sighed.

He arrived at the gift shop in tennis shoes without socks, a thin sweater, and damped hair. He looked desperate to find something. He looked around before asking the salesman.

"Are these the only ties you have?" He asked impatiently.

The salesman frowned "Unfortunately, that's all we have."

He rolled his eyes and headed out the door.

"For your information, there is a store on the corner." He twisted his lips in a girlish manner and moved his hands like he had a broken wrist. His well-manicured glossy nails were moving in every direction. When they finally stopped in the direction of the store, Na Min bolted out of the gift shop saying, "Thanks!"

He found the store to be closed, "No! No! No!" He stood there as the cold air gave him a chill. He danced a little to keep warm. He held his hands in front of his mouth to warm them. He looked up at the sky as the snowflakes fell. Suddenly he saw a saleswoman pass, "Hey!" He tapped on the glass door and frantically pointed at his watch. "What time do you open?" He could feel his toes starting to get cold.

She walked over to the door and smiled; one of those pseudo retail smiles. "Fifteen minutes!" she yelled through the glass doors and pointed at the clock on the wall.

He shivered and lowered his head, "I... do I look like I can wait fifteen more minutes?"

She thought he was cute, and desperate to get inside from the elements. She looked at her watch and the clock on the wall, "You have to wait fifteen more minutes." She walked away.

He pulled his badge and tapped it hard on the glass. He was frustrated. She turned around, but the badge changed her attitude. She looked at him and felt sorry for him. She threw up both of her hands and said, "The key."

She returned a couple of seconds later, bent down like a lady with her knees together and upper body twisted to accommodate her position. Before she turned the key she asked, "Let me see that badge again... I know a fake one when I see one." The sound of the key unlocked the door. The cold air rushed in and the sound of the early morning commute filtered into the store.

"Oh thank you so much." He stood there to brush off the snowflakes and tried to get comfortable in the heated store.

"What are you doing without a coat?" the saleswoman asked.

He interrupted her, "I need a tie...preferred." He said with a gesture of urgency. He still held his hands to his mouth.

She felt ignored. "Yes, we have some blue ties."

"You have no idea how important this is to me. I thank you from the bottom of my heart." He followed her toward the suits and ties.

The saleswoman was a beautiful 5'6, dark-eyed, curly-haired Puerto Rican, the shape was to die for and her accent was a sniper in the bush and she admired him for some reason. "I take it you have an important meeting you have to go to?" she asked cunningly as she flirted.

He was so into finding the perfect tie. He hadn't noticed her gestures. "What about these ties?" He turned to look at her. "Is that... well, that's not the only tie you have... is it?" He impatiently searched for another suitable tie. He frantically looked at his watch, "Damn! You..."

"Listen..." she interrupted him. "Hey, I have more ties in the back that I guarantee you would not walk out of here without."

Moments later she returned with an arm filled with some of the most beautiful ties in the world. "Nowhere are..." she was interrupted.

"You have to help me. My wife shops for my ties..." he said carefully holding two ties in the air for comparison.

She smirked and picked out the most expensive tie. Her attitude changed from a flirting to a disappointed one, the voice became tolerating than a helping one. "Well..." she picked out a blue tie, "...this is your tie that you have to buy. It can be worn with any suit. The colors that twine in between..."

He stopped her. "Excuse me, I am so sorry, but I have to really be somewhere. Just charge it to my credit card." He put his credit card on the glass counter.

"Do you have I.D.?" she asked.

He showed her his C.I.A. badge and identification. "Do you have state I.D.?"

He impatiently reached for his wallet, "Here!" He rudely put it on the glass instead of her hand and sighed with frustration.

She looks at it, comparing the two.

He combed his fingers through his jet black hair and rolled his eyes.

"Aah, …how much is it?"

She pulled the tag from the back of the tie and cleared her throat, "Eight hundred dollars and forty-three cents." She frowned and he almost passed out.

"What! Eight hundred dollars and forty-three cents." he looked at the clock.

"This is not the cheapest tie you have!" He panicked as he almost pulled his hair out.

"Well… you did ask for red…," she pushed her lips upward and forced herself to smile. "And this is the last tie that we have." before she could say another word.

"Just charge it." He told himself that he would most definitely bring it back. He shook his head as the machine made all kinds of noise as it printed the receipt. He wanted to reach over and choke this bitch, but it was not her fault, besides he had just noticed how cute her accent was. She was beautiful, her makeup was flawless, teeth were pearly white; she used her right index to specifically scratch in one spot of her scalp.

She held his credit card closer to her face to read his name, "Mr. Choi." He nodded his head.

"Not many people can pronounce it." He looked at her name tag and said her name with the proper Spanish accent.

She was shocked, "wow…"

He stopped her before she could ask. "It's a good chance that I speak Spanish better than you."

She handed him his credit card and I.D. with his bag with the tie in it. He quickly said goodbye and dashed out of the store with his credit card and receipt between his lips. A snowflake touched his eyebrow, the cold winter elements rushed him as he hurried back to the hotel, being occupied with putting everything back in his wallet and the sound of the snow crunched after every step. Thinking it was dumb of him to leave without a jacket. He wanted to make it back to eat breakfast with his family, something he had not done in three years.

Kandace heard a knock at the door, "Who is it?"

She walked towards the door.

"It's room service."

The kids got excited, "Ok kids, it's time to eat breakfast."

"Where is Daddy? Cynthia asked.

"He should be back soon."

Kandace opened the door, "Good morning."

The waiter pushed the cart into the room, "You have to sign here Ma'am." He gave her the bill.

"Is that it?" she asked.

"Yes Ma'am, enjoy." She gave him a tip and closed the door behind him.

"OK Justin!" she arranged the table, "Come have a seat at the table." She pushed the cart and the table closer to the window as they gathered around.

"Mommy, can I have extra bacon?" Cynthia asked.

Down below, Na Min was a hundred feet from the entrance to the Marriott. Suddenly, the explosion vibrated the surrounding buildings, shattering windows across the street. He fell to his knees as debris of glass and brick hit him. The people on the street panicked; nearby car alarms sounded, people ran for their lives. He stood and wiped his eyes and noticed he was bleeding. He looked up at the hotel and saw that it was his hotel room that had exploded. He screamed.

"Noooo!" he looked on the ground and saw one of his son's shoes. He folded. "Nooooo!" he cried. The smoke from the hotel burned. He looked around and ran to his daughter. He was having a difficult time swallowing his pain. He held her and cried. She was dead. She was missing an arm and a leg.

"Cynthia! Cynthia!" he held her close. He tried mouth-to-mouth resuscitation. She was gone. He screamed at the top of his lungs, "Why!" He yelled in Korean.

"Kandace! Justin!" He stood up and frantically searched. He was covered in his daughter's blood. His tears fell and choked him. His wife lay on top of the hood of a taxi. He ran over to her with a loss for words. He touched her, her eyes opened. "Help is on the way!"

She cried and held him while she went into shock. He was so nervous; he couldn't think straight. Her legs were gone and blood pumped out. He carried her from the hood of the taxi to the sidewalk. She grabbed him, "Justin!" She tried to scream. Her voice was cracked and low. She grabbed her chest and frowned. She had a puncture wound to her lungs. "Justin... save my boy!" she pointed.

He looked in the direction that she pointed. He ran over, but it was too late. "Justin! Don't you die on me! No!" he picked him up and carried him to his mother. He looked fine, but he had a puncture wound to his heart.

"Cynthia!?" she asked.

He cried as the sirens got closer. She took her last breath. Justin died moments later, no longer bothered by the cold winter morning. His anger heated him. He slammed his fist onto the sidewalk until his knuckles bled. He rested on his knees; he slowly forced his hands to come to his face. "Our father ..." he prayed for the first time in five years. He fell forward as he mumbled the Lord's Prayer out of his mouth. He collapsed to the sidewalk, curled like an infant; the love of his life was snatched from him. He had wished he had died. He never recovered mentally from this loss.

He sat there at his desk holding a family photo. His wet eyes were evidence that he could not hide from his current wife; she walked into his office.

"Honey, are you ok?" She stood at the door.

"Yeah." He picked up his glass of Genifer and took a sip and sighed. She knew there were times he would go through a moment of depression, especially, when he thought about his kids, and she was unable to bare any. She walked over and kissed him on the lips. He looked at the photo of Kalargo when he was fourteen in his martial art class. He was so proud of him, and most of all, that he had adopted him. They cut the lights out and walked out of the office.

Chapter Thirteen

Seoul, South Korea

One year had passed after the hotel bombing, "Did you meet your contact? He asked.

Bradley sighed, scratched his eyebrow, he exhaled the visible hot breath from his mouth and nose. His scarf was wrapped around his neck. He stomped his feet and rubbed his hands. It was very cold; they both looked like Michelin men under their clothes. He blew on his hands to keep them warm. He opened the back door of the fish market and Agent Bradley followed.

Agent Bradley was born Korean American working deep cover in South Korea and North Korea as a C.I.A. operative. He looked one hundred percent Korean and spoke their language with no foreign accent. Both of his parents were born in South Korea and he had lived in Seoul, South Korea until the age of fourteen. He was very comfortable being in his home country, among his family helped blend him in very well. But he and his daughter lived in the United States. He was older than Na Min, but he looked up to him as a hero. He had heard of the Central America interrogations. He felt like he was working with a legend.

The 10 degrees below zero weather chilled them to their bones. They sighed after the door was closed and stood there and let the heat absorb their faces before they stomped the ice from their boots. He looked at

him with this stupid look on his face before he smiled. "Yes!" he said
with an excited but low tone of voice. "I have…" he pulled him aside and
reached in his pocket. "He showed him a roll of film. "Launchpads,
bases, missile storage, and…" They quickly changed the subject as a
worker walked past them. He slowly slid the roll of film back into his
pocket. They took their coats off and hung them on the coat hooks.

"Are you guys working or chatting for a paycheck?" the supervisor
asked them both.

They remained in character, "We work for our checks boss!"

"I'll believe it when I see it."

"You are on table one and Na Min takes table three, Kim can't make it
today." Their supervisor walked away.

Before they separated Bradley pulled him by his shirt and whispered,
"Our tunnels are complete; we can go into the north whenever we want
now."

A loud voice in Korean came over the loudspeaker, "Hey we need
more eel head and octopus heart!"

"Right on it!" He yelled back, smiled, and sighed at his flawless
Korean.

"Yeah and guess what..." he leaned towards him, looking away a
moment. Na Min's butcher knife cut open a baby octopus in half. He
frowned and could not stand his deep cover assignment.

"They are making a submarine that carries nukes." They both chopped up eels and octopuses. The smell of the sea no longer bothered them.

"We need to get over there and take photos." Na Min said.

Bradley pulled out a small folded paper with his fingertips, carefully to not get blood on it. "Check this out." he raised his eyebrows. "Wow, tell me this is not what I think it is?" he quickly shoved it in his back pocket."Six months, it will be completed."

"How did you get this?" Na Min looked at him strangely. He always tried to impress him; he knew it would do exactly that and also bring him closer to his death.

"Another thing, this job has to go!" he pointed his long pointy knife at him.

He laughed, "This is where I get all of my drops."

"Eel, octopus ready!" Na Min said.

"If it's not broke, don't fix it." Bradley looked at him.

"Whale eyes, ready!" Bradley said.

The sound of their stainless steel knives can be heard chopping away.

"This needs to be cut in smaller portions!" the head fisherman said. They looked at each other, and then at the packaged fish.

"This is it." they both reached for it. Bradley grabbed it first. They looked around the kitchen suspiciously. He ran his hand in between the guts of this huge eel. He felt something.

"Yes, this is it." he pulled out a roll of film that had been wrapped in plastic.

Bradley had this nervous feeling that he had never felt before.

Na Min wiped his forehead with the inside of his sweaty forearm. He held his butcher knife in his left hand. They smiled.

"Good work. Damn good work, but I could not have done it without..." he kind of nodded his head to the left. "...may be hurting someone." They both smiled.

Six months later

"This is good, look at this." Na Min looked at the negative at an angle above his head; holding it between his fingertips.

"Beautiful. They are going to slobber all over these." Bradley said.

Their safe house was close to the DMZ (demilitarized zone).

The Korean War never really ended between the south and the north. For almost twenty years they have been at war. But not a bullet has been fired. The Americans and South Koreans stand guard all day, every day. It is so intense around the DMZ, no one is allowed to smile, show fear, or help the enemy. The white paint that separates the south from the north is twelve inches in width. The soldiers are always at attention or in the ready position.

"Yep, this is definitely what they are looking for," he said as he held another negative towards the ceiling.

"OK, tomorrow would be a good time to go to Seoul," Bradley said.

"You want me to make reservations?" Na Min asked.

"Yes." He holds a negative in each hand up to the light.

The following day

Seoul, South Korea

"Yes, how can I help you?" a beautiful Korean asked. "Hmm, yes we have two rooms reserved for five nights." the sound of the computer keys tapped away.

"Do you have identification?" she smiled, her straight black hair past her elbows, no cleavage, but her blue suit fitted her well. She turned away to code their room keys. Her calves were thick, and hips flat. "OK gentlemen, your rooms are across from one another. If you need any assistance dial seven, for room service dial eight, and for emergencies dial nine." she pushed the keys across the counter. She ripped the receipt from the printer. "And you must sign... here, and here." she pointed at both of the receipts.

Bradley looked at his watch, "Still early, first thing first, I'll run over to the base..." he touched his watch.

"I'll find Mr. Bonjivich to develop these negs."

"We'll meet back here at nineteen hundred hours." They both agreed and separated into their rooms.

1830 hundred hours

Na Min returned early, slowly slid in his key, the light blinked, the sound of the lock unlocked. He struggled to retrieve his key for a moment. The door opened. The beige carpet matched the bedspread and the contrast of wallpaper said a lot about the interior designer. He had to be drunk or blind, but the hotel was super clean and dated.

He rushed toward the bathroom as he began to remove some of his clothes, unbuckle his pants; he passed the television, queen-size bed, office desk, and the old rusty iron heater. He thought he would have gotten down to the third layer of clothes by now.

"God damn it!" He danced, wiggled his way around the bathroom floor, still not ready, he held his legs together. He unzipped, pulled four sweaters upward, finally he stood still long enough to urinate everywhere but in the toilet. "Jesus Christ!" his aim was just a little off. He cleaned the mess that he made and sighed as he walked out of the bathroom.

"Hmmm... Bradley must have left something for me." The brown paper bag was wrapped tightly with yellow rubber bands around it. No note. He sniffed it for bomb materials. He grabbed one of his shoes and stood halfway in the bathroom, aimed, and threw the shoe at it. "Nothing." he thought.

He scratched his ear, forehead, and stomach before approaching the bed. Before he picked the package up, he scratched again. He did this scratching thing every time he got nervous. Slowly, one rubber band at a time he removed them. After the fourth rubber band, the sound of the paper bag begins to unravel. He peeked; looked, put his right hand in the bag that would change the rest of his life. It will cause him to lie, spy, and do what he never thought he would do in a lifetime. This would be the beginning of crossing the line of integrity. He had two chances to turn back. He didn't.

His bottom jaw dropped. What he held in his hand caused his fingers to tremble. He ran to the door and peeped through the peephole for fifty-nine seconds.

"What the hell is going on?" he asked himself as he peeped through the peephole. He walked over to the bed and shoved it in the pillowcase. He sweated heavily; he took off his layer of clothing. With just his light blue boxers on, he tiptoed to the door again.

"Nobody!" he acted like a drug addict. He looked through the peephole for a hundred thirty-two seconds. He felt like someone was watching him. He took his eye from the peephole, looked at his watch. "Where is he? It's eighteen thirty-five..." He saw Bradley walk up to his door. His heart pounded his chest like wild apes. Bradley dropped his key, but he finally got into his room.

Na Min watched for a while to make sure he was not followed, thinking the phone would ring in his hotel; he hoped he would call him soon. He stood dumbfounded with his back against the door. He curled his toes into the carpet. His palms itched and his armpits perspired. He closed his eyes and waited. "This has to be a joke, a test, but why?" he asked himself. He dug his nails into his palms trying to cure the itch. The knock at the door startled him. He peeped through the peephole. He opened the door and the room lit up from the hallway light.

Bradley entered the room with just the bathroom light on. "Na Min... well damn it's dark in here." He walked over to the dresser and flicked on the nightstand light.

He stood there in his light blue boxers with Winnie the Pooh printed on them. "So how was your day?" he asked with a little curiosity.

Bradley took a load off of his feet." I talked to what's his name... and it's a go." he put out his cigarette in the ashtray. "I got everything lined up for Tuesday. The u-2 should be able to get some better photos to confirm this submarine facility," he said as he cleared his throat.

Na Min slid into his pants, right leg first. He hoped he would ask about the package on the bed. Maybe he had one on his bed that he was curious about.

Years later, he will wish he had asked about it.

"Well, my end should be good to go. I dropped off the negs." Suddenly he yawned. "Boy, I am getting tired. What time in the morning?" Na Min asked him.

"It'll be a late start... go ahead and get some rest." Bradley stood up and headed towards the door.

"Hey just call me." Na Min said.

"Will do." the door closed behind him.

Five days later

Bradley and Na Min stood in the lobby of their hotel talking to a couple of Army officers.

166

"That gets me every time..." An officer said. They spoke about Vietnam. Their bodies were tipsy of liquor as they leaned on each other.

"So you boys are headed back to the DMZ in the morning?" Bradley asked them.

"Well, unfortunately, we are. Shit, to be honest, I can't wait to go back to Stateside." He expressed with the hands of a flying airplane landing on his palm. Their Rum had kicked in a while ago.

"Well..." looking at his watch, "...this old fart must head in." Na Min shook hands and said his goodbyes.

Later he entered his hotel room nervously. He quickly closed the door. He looked at the bed and felt like falling to the floor, another package on his bed. "Damn, damn, damn..." he sighed. He used both of his hands to cover his face and slowly dragged them down his chin. He no longer looked through the peephole. His alcohol slowly reduced its effect. The party was over. The reality was smacking him in the face. This was the fourth package. He was pretty sure that the content is the same as before, fifteen thousand dollars American. It made him more nervous that he had not said anything. He opened it. He sighed. He felt like any moment there would be agents rushing into his room to arrest him, including Agent Bradley.

"Oh my God, what am I getting myself into" he looked up at the ceiling. He grabbed the package and threw it against the wall, knocking over a flower pot.

There was a note, and photos that lay on the floor among the money. He felt like throwing up. This is the classic case of blackmail. He looked at the picture of him passing a newspaper to a known foreign national. It looked like he was doing nothing wrong. The next picture was of him counting a huge amount of money in the hotel room. He felt like he was trapped, cornered.

He read the note, "Hello... there is no way out. We have you counting your money, exchanging documents, which contain secrets. Meet me at the coffee shop across the street in the morning at eight am."

He balds the note up into his palm and gritted his teeth. His left eyelid twitches when his blood pressure rises, and it twitches non-stop. He sighed deeply as he just let his body fall back onto the bed. He grabbed the bedspread with his hands and covered his face. He knew he had not betrayed his country, but he felt guilty, looked guilty, and if it got out that he is a trader. He would die without the honor of a true American hero.

* * *

Pyongyang, North Korea

Two years later

"I can't do this!" Na Min sat in the old mildew-smelling apartment. The firewood crackles every once in a while as the snow falls outside. He sat in a chair surrounded by four North Korean secret servicemen. Their sweaters came up to their chins; their heavy-duty snow boots were still wet from the melted snow. "I just can't do it anymore. I rather die, I've given you enough!" Na Min said.

The room was silent. The ruby-red curtains missed links at the top where it hung horribly.

"Listen, you must not understand your position?" One of them walked over to him. "Smoke?" He was short but cocky.

"No!" he stood up to leave, snatching his coat from the back of his chair.

"We own you..." his voice had a lot of respect when he spoke. He walked forward and the others stepped back. He came from the darkest part of the room, like a ghost, "...for treason, you will get the death penalty!" he pulled the chair and repositioned it.

Na Min's hand was on the doorknob.

"Relax, so far so good, no one knows anything about your treason." He smiled.

With his head down, he wished he could commit suicide, just get it over with." And who are you?" he let go of the doorknob.

"No one has to know." he spoke with an assuring voice."You are one of the highest-ranking agents that we have on our payroll. Is it the money? OK, we'll give you more of it, but..." He pushed the chair towards him and pointed at it, "...sit the fuck down!" For that one split second, he sounded like an American.

"I will never! Never allow you to walk free!" He spoke with this calm and collective voice."You have moved up in rank. We want secrets, and shipments going to The Gambia."

He stood in front of him with his fingers interlocked. He placed his hands on his face and looked him in his eyes. "We are going to colonize The Gambia, Africa. We have knowledge that there are minerals and if we can take over the country, it would bring more revenue..." he pointed his index finger at him. "...with your ability, you would be able to help ship weapons to help overthrow this country."

"Your ass belongs to me wherever you are in the world!" his voice was bone-chilling. The vibration of his words melted his spirits. He felt like a trader.

"Who are you?" Na Min bravely asked.

"My name is Agent Zang." he stood up and walked over to the window with his hands behind his back. The hole on the side of his head, ear burned off, and his skin-tight on his face, making him frown. "Now, let us continue this beautiful relationship." he looked over his shoulder to look at this powerless man that had once killed, tortured, spat on others and abused his enemy. He held his head up, but his dignity and shame were like a first-time abused dog with his tail between his legs. He sighed.

"Can I have something to drink?" Make it strong, no ice, straight." he whispered like a scary bitch that had been down in a pit of darkness and begged to be pulled out. He felt like he had to behave, cooperate or face the consequences.

For two hours he paid close attention to their plans for Africa, nicknamed, "The Program" Finally the meeting was over; he had his new mission of being a double agent for the North Koreans. One by one they walked out of the apartment. In came two transporters to take him back to South Korea. They walked him down the stairs to the parking garage. The driver was ready. He got in the back seat as the two transporters sat to his left and right. As this small dusty red four-door car pulled out into the street. "Here." the driver reached around and tossed him a blue eyeless hood so he would not see the way to and from their underground tunnel that they use to travel from North Korea to South Korea. It took years to build this twenty-mile tunnel to

South Korea to a house in a small farm town.

Back at the safe house in South Korea, Na Min stood at the window overlooking the street as Bradley walked across the street for the second time to mail a letter off to his sister that lived in Chicago. Maybe it was strange, but not unusual. He often mailed letters to his daughter, Yuki. So it didn't cross his mind to ask him about it.

* * *

Present day

He came back to reality from a daydream that wet the corner of his eyes.
In front of him sat a bottle of Gin and a glass half full. The blueberry
candles scented the room. He sighed as he put his family picture back in
its place, near the far corner of his desk in front of him. He always
wished that he could turn back the clock. He would have never invited
his wife and kids to Washington D.C. He looked at his glorious painting
of himself. He frowned in disgust at how he became. But the money was
so plentiful; it made him comfortable and led him into the mind frame
that it was OK.

He reached for his glass and slowly put it to his lips. The taste soothed
his pain, heeled his inner scars instantly. It justified his past. He nodded
his head and agreed; "It's going to be OK." he looked at the entrance to
his office. His current wife walked in looking just as beautiful as the day
he bought the tie. He was excited by her presence. He stood up and
paused. He stumbled forward.

She came to his aid." Baby, you are drunk again." she put her shoulder
underneath his left arm for support. "Well, it's time for bed. They
staggered step by step. He twisted his fingers in her shiny black curly
hair. Her Spanish accent thundered his left ear. "Come on," she said.

With his lips, he made the sound of a vacuum, "Vroooom vrooom."

She laughed and grinned. He rubbed her breast softly." Just a little
further..." they stumbled a little, "...and you are in no shape to do that."

She pushed him onto the bed. Took off his shoes, socks, pants, and noticed that he had a violent hard-on, "Yeah, you go to sleep."

He rubbed her thigh and tried to kiss her weak spot, the back of her ear. She whacks his hard-on hard, he fell onto the bed. "Not fair! That hurt!" he slurred his drunken words. Finally, she rolled him onto his stomach and covers him with the bedsheet.

* * *

The phone rings several times before Zang could hang up, "Hello, Jenko how are the Philippines?" his voice filled the earpiece.

"Just fine, no complaints, doing some paperwork," Jenko said.

"Did you get a chance to talk to Kalargo?" Zang asked, there was a pause in the conversation.

"Why!" he asked.

"Well, I thought he would have contacted you. I mean he has been in the Philippines for a month already."

"What!"

"He was down in the southern islands of the Philippines for training. He was busy, but he did come through Manila International airport."

Jenko sighed, not really caring that much about it. He never really got along with him. But put up a front to do business with him. He could not

173

stand Kalargo and no one knew this deep animosity. "Well, you know how that Bruce Lee wannabe is." Jenko had to throw that comment into the conversation.

Zang thought back to when Kalargo had defeated him so many times in their Karate competition. He never could defeat him. For years he hated him, but their friendship grew despite the browns, yellows, and blue belts of martial arts. The leadership capability that they exhibited was proof that secured their future with Zang and Na Min. Between the two of them, they divided the Asian Pacific, Kalargo supplied weapons to Africa and South America. Jenko supplied weapons to Thailand, Burma, Vietnam, the Philippines, Laos, Singapore, and Indonesia. For many years, first place or second, they remain friends and share information between the two of them. However, as teens, the bitter taste that he had for him remained at the bottom of his throat. He learned to deal with his issues and grew out of it, but it left a dark side to him.

Jenko stood 5'8, a hundred eighty-five pounds with a caramel chocolate complexion, and almond eyes from his dad, who was a Korean American. His clean-shaven model physique gave him a boost among the Philippine community, but his status in martial arts gave him an ultimate high. His premiere opening to his martial arts training facility was a huge success. Deep down inside he did not really want to listen to all this crap, but he did anyway since they were associated for many years.

"Well, basically I am calling to congratulate you on your business venture. I wish you all well."

"Thank you, will there be any other shipments?" Jenko asked.

"No, but if anything pops up I will definitely let you know. I'll keep in touch." And they both said their goodbyes.

He was so happy to get off the phone. He gritted his teeth until his veins and muscles showed through his neck and face. He slammed the receiver down and felt like he owed him something. The money was good, war has always been a booming business and so far, there was no looking back. Jenko stood in his office holding a picture of him and his mother. He tossed it aside rather than hanging it up. He wanted his mother to witness his success, not hear about it. He grabbed it again and walked towards a file cabinet along the back wall that had over twenty trophies, another fifteen were placed in the front of the training facility for display of experience. He bent down to pull the bottom drawer. He stopped before tossing it, with his left hand he picked up an unframed photo. He looked at it and sighed. He was sixteen years old and stood next to a trophy that was taller than him. The photo also had Kalargo standing next to him with a first-place trophy that stood taller than his trophy. That was the last competition they participated in. He placed it back in the drawer and decided to hang the photo of him and his mom on the wall.

"Right here…" held the nail and tapped it with a small hammer. He proudly hung the photo and made sure that it was perfect.

* * *

Seoul, South Korea 1970's

Mugumbi meets Na Min

"Listen, my stepfather is a reputable man in South Korea if anyone can help you, he can," Yuki said to Mugumbi in his native language Jola.

Mugumbi and Tipi had been in South Korea for several months. He looked for work, but the language barrier got in the way. They both sat in a small bar about ten blocks away from a military base. He slowly sipped his cocktail. There were a handful of Koreans and most Americans that frequented the bar. An occasional regular would walk in and take a seat. His dark complexion and features gave him a non-American look. So he couldn't really blend in as an American. Some of them who had been stationed there long enough had the privilege of speaking Korean. The music blared off Micheal Jackson," "ABC ".

The darkness of the bar would spook a stranger but normalize a regular customer.

"Mugumbi, listen to me." The bar door opened and the daylight illuminated the bar briefly. They looked to see who was entering. The voices of the bar welcomed a regular, "Bill!" They raised their glasses to him. He walked over to his favorite part of the bar and lifted his wrist at everyone. His hand was blown off during the Korean War by a grenade.

"Yuki…" he leaned back on the stool. His jet black African features highly defined his culture, nose, lips, Afro, and being in South Korea was as strange as a snake wearing a jean jacket to keep warm. He felt like the main attraction, a freak at times. People would literally want and often touch his skin out of curiosity. They want to see if the makeup would rub off.

"Yuki, how are you able to speak my native language Jola? I felt so lost before I met you." He held her hand. "Now, it's almost like I am dependent on you. Can you teach me your language?"

She lit a cigarette and puffed, blew the smoke away from his face, leaned over, and locked her lips on to his, "Of course, I will. You want to learn English also?" she smiled and puffed until the cherry of her cigarette couldn't get any brighter. "As far as how I speak your native tongue…" she paused and looked down at his hands, "…my biological father moved to Africa and I lived there for four years. I had a nanny that taught me to read and write." She took a sip of her drink and played with the ends of her hair. "Let's just say that…" she looked him in his eyes, "…someone else was more serious about me learning the language than I was ever interested." They both laughed.

"Well I can truly say she did a good job" he sips on his drink. He slowly looked at his half-empty glass and slowly put it down. He sighed. "What happened to your father?"

She turned her head and pushed her hair out of her face.

"If you prefer not to talk about it, I would totally understand." He held her hand.

"No, no, I mean it's not that. Just thinking of him and the memories that I do have of him…" she downed her drink, "…he was everything;

my father gave me the security that I looked for. You know. That protection that nothing would happen to me."

"Well, he's an American hero." She smiled. "He died in a gunfight in Osan. He tried to save my stepfather in a shootout. Just before he died he told his partner…"

"Another drink?" the bartender was ready to refill their glass.

"Yes, two." Mugumbi agreed with two fingers. "Yeah, I don't want to be nervous when your stepfather gets here."

"Tequila, coming up!"

"Yes," he looked at her. "That means yes?" he asked her. "I will learn Korean, just give me some time."

She waved her hands in front of her face as if she forgets where she had ended the story about her father.

"What kind of work your father did," he asked her. "Logistics business?" She looked at his dried lower lip. She placed her index finger on his chin and played with his clit tickler, the small patch of hair below his lower lip curled outward. Just before she spoke, she sneezed.

"God bless." He gave her a napkin.

"Well, he traveled a lot." She wiped her nose and moved in closer to his face with her slanted eyes, high cheekbone, and pale face. Her thin lips touched his lips, even though he was not attractive, but she liked him. Finally, she found something to say. She ignored his question.

178

"So anyway, long story short…" she interrupted him, but before she could get a word out. The door opened and a burst of outside light entered the bar. She looked over her shoulder and it was Na Min standing there searching with his eyes. There was no huge welcome for him. He wasn't a regular. "Oh no…" Yuki said.

"What?" Mugumbi looked at the door.

She stood from her stool. It was obvious that he had arrived. The alcohol was not working like he had thought it would. He quickly slammed his drink down his throat and pounded his fist on his chest. He frowned, gagged, and exhaled the burning sensation of the Tequila from his throat.

She waved him towards them. Their smiles were mutual. She stood and bowed slightly. He felt obliged to do the same.

Na Min reached out and gave her a hug.

"Daddy this is Mugumbi." She pointed her hands towards Mugumbi.

He looked at him and nodded his head, "So you are the lucky man I have been hearing about." He reached his right hand out and shook his hand. "I have heard about your journey from Africa, amazing." He spoke to them in English. Yuki translated every word to him.

"I am a very busy man, but whatever I can do to help on behalf of my daughter." He took a seat and waved his hand to the bartender, "Gin please."

"He needs work. He doesn't speak Korean, but he speaks some English." She looked at her stepfather.

He let out a huge sigh and sipped from his glass. "He needs a miracle."

"But you make miracles happen all the time." She grabbed Mugumbi by the arm.

"Most of my miracles start with the same language. This is different. This is South Korea."

"Oh yeah, he also has a nephew that came along." She said with a hesitant smile.

Na Min looked at her, "Damn, what did you do, inherit these people?" he sighed and rubbed his eyes with both hands. He looked at Mugumbi. There were questions he wanted to ask, but not in front of Yuki.

He looked at them both, and mentally asked "Can this guy be trusted? There is only one way to find out." He rubbed his eyes and nodded his head to the left. "I tell you what; I may be able to get him some work as a dishwasher." He looked at him. "I know some people that might hire him." He picked up his drink and held up to toast. Their glasses cling as they touch.

He licked his dry lips and smiled. He extended his hand, and they shook on it. Out of respect, Mugumbi bowed. "Thank you, thank you."

"Mugumbi, I am an American. So shaking my hand is apart from my culture." They laughed.

"I will call you in the morning." They agreed.

He reached into his faded blue jeans and pulled out money to pay the tab for them both. "Bartender, keep the change!" he said out loud. He kissed Yuki on the cheek and rubbed her on her back. He said his goodbyes and walked away into the darkness of the bar. The burst of light filled the bar as the door opened, darkness resumed as the door closed.

Chapter Fourteen

"Yuki, listen I have a translator for him. He'll be there to pick him up. Tell him to be ready in an hour" he slowly put the phone on the receiver.

The blue sky carried a breeze from the east at 10 mph. periodically the smell of the bread bakery not far away from her small apartment lingered. The mixture of eggs, bacon, and grits clashed with the sweet bakery bread.

"Mugumbi!" her childlike voice from the kitchen.

"Yeah," he responded from the bedroom.

"Your ride will be here in an hour." She stirred the eggs.

Kalargo slept on the floor beneath the blanket. The sound of voices awakens him. He opened his eyes to the smell of food, stretched his little body, and rubbed his eyes. "I am hungry."

Mugumbi entered the living room, "I have an interview for a job."

Kalargo rolled over.

"Are you hungry?" she asked. Just like a kid, his head popped through the blanket.

"Breakfast is served." She put the plates on the table.

The translator knocked on the door.

"One moment…" Yuki peeped through the peephole.

"Well, he's here." She kissed him on his lips, with her teeth; she held his lower lip in a romantic vice grip. A small amount of saliva oozed from their mouths for a sloppy kiss goodbye.

"Hey." The translator extended his hand out. "Good morning…" with a smile, "…my name is Bogig for short, Bo. Na Min wants me to teach you Korean, show you around town."

Bo had an earring of a cross with diamonds around it, small but cute, a super thick mustache, with a failed attempt to dye his gray hairs. "I am not sure what job you will have, but whatever it is, do your best, because there are better positions." He led the way to his car.

Mugumbi walked towards the left side of the car and opened the door. "First I have to learn Korean." The sound of the engine roared. "This is a nice ride." He complimented his five-year-old '74 Isuzu.

"Seat belts… well, believe me, if they like you, they will send you to school for whatever you need to learn. When I first came here fifteen years ago, I spoke no Korean and I got a break washing dishes. Everything went uphill from that point on. Hopefully…" he was interrupted by his cell phone. His Korean was almost flawless. He was amazed by how well he spoke. After three minutes on the phone, Bo flipped his left traffic signal. "Well, I have a pit stop to make." Their conversation continued.

The storefronts and street signs were all foreign to him; traffic drove on the right side of the street. It appeared that every Korean in the country had a bicycle. Driving through small narrow roads, squeezing alongside park cars, they arrived at the back of an apartment building and parked.

"Now what?" Mugumbi asked.

Bo pulled out a box of cigarettes, "Smoke?"

"Why not." he leaned over to use his flame from his match that had burned halfway down its stem.

"In about five minutes…" Bo inhaled his smoke. He turned the radio down a little, "…a white guy will drop off an envelope. The alarm lights will flash on that brown Toyota to let us know the package is ready for pick up. Even though we may not see this guy, I know he's an American, and military. But what matters is that we get the package and deliver it." The front two windows were rolled down.

They both exhaled a cloud of smoke. He paid close attention to his surroundings. Bo bloodshot eyes; rough black skin tone gave him a sinister look. He stood 5'7, 215 pounds, mostly around his waist, and buttocks.

"So I guess we are like a carrier service, pick up and deliver?" Mugumbi asked.

Bo flicked the ashes out the window and laughed. "If that's how you see it. Yeah, I guess, in a way."

The alarm sounded on the Toyota and Bo opened his car door. "I'll be right back."

Moments later, the interior lights came on and Bo was back with an envelope. "Now we can go." He tossed it on the back seat. "Now I can take you where you need to be." He started the car and drove off.

The rest of the day went smooth, eventually coming to an end. "Mugumbi! Wake up!" he nudged his shoulder, "Get yourself together." Bo shifted the gear to park.

He exhaled hard. "I'm up…" he opened his eyes and looked around, "…damn, where are we?"

"We are here. Listen, if this guy likes you. You'll have a job." Bo pointed his finger at him.

Mugumbi turned and leaned to the left, quickly licked the back of his index finger to check for bad breath. "Damn…" he frowned. "…doing what?"

Bo took the keys out of the ignition. "Just be happy to have a job, this is Korea, the job chooses us."

He sighed and crossed his fingers. They parked in a parking garage two blocks away.

"Wow, this is downtown?" Mugumbi looked amazed.

They approached one of the tallest buildings in the downtown area. The streets were packed with pedestrians and bicycles. He just could not get over how many bicycles neatly lined the street. He looked up at the clock read 12pm.

"Right here," Bo said.

He paused and looked upward. "Wow."

"Well here goes everything." He pulled one of the quadruple glass doors. The emblem of an eye that covered the marble floor, above it was Net Rem Grat Services. He stood still as people bumped into him.

"Come on," Bo said.

"The elevators are over here." He pointed into the direction. Upon entering the building, two Korean women bowed at them. They bowed back.

"Ding ding." The elevator doors closed as the last person squeezed his way in.

"Hey, pressed the eighteenth floor," Bo said.

The elevators were not spared from top-notch decorating, oak wood, and velvet. Coming from Africa, this was definitely first class. The crowd looked shy but whispered among themselves. They giggled.

"What are they saying?" Mugumbi asked.

Bo smiled, "You don't want to know."

"Hey… you are supposed to teach me."

Bo grinned and looked at him, "Let's just say that they admire how dark we are." He rubbed the back of his hand. "Our lips are so big." He closed his mouth and exhaled hard enough so his lips would purposely vibrate. Three of the women burst into giggles behind the palms of their hands that covered their mouths.

"Ding ding." The women walked off on the eleventh floor.

"Seven more floors to go," Bo said.

They exited the elevator and the vanilla fragrance tickled their nose. The receptionist stood and bowed, "Good afternoon"

In huge gold plated letters, "Net Rem Grat services inc." on a reddish-orange wall that said, "We deliver when they say it's impossible."

The wall-to-wall gray carpet felt like cotton beneath their feet. The marble and oak gave an affluent atmosphere.

"Yes, we have an appointment." Bo leaned on the counter that was up to his chest.

After she bowed again she pushed two bottoms on the computer, and one on the phone. The voice on the loudspeaker was cut short when she picked the receiver up.

"Yes…" as she spoke on the phone.

Mugumbi walked over to the miniature statues and paintings, one by one. The oldest one of them all, he felt obliged to touch. It was a South Korean miniature forest with a waterfall that fogged at the bottom of the mini pawn. The sound of falling water echoed the pawn as it fell. He looked at the bottom of the pool of water and saw some strange objects that appeared to be dirty stones. Just before he dipped his hand, he noticed a sign in Korean.

"Bo, what does this say?" his finger pointed.

Bo strolled over with his hands behind his back. His lips mumbled. "Well, it says high voltage. Try at your own risk."

"Excuse me, sir." The receptionist called. "He will be with you in a moment."

They took their seats in the waiting area. They looked at the magazines. Clients entered and left for four hours. Mugumbi dozed off, tried to fight off Sandman, but he looked as if he was being kicked around, his head bobbing back and forward. He tried to rest his head to the left and tried to find a good position every twenty minutes. The magazine he held had fallen between his legs and woke him up. He opened his eyes to look around to see if anyone was watching. He saw Bo standing and flirting with the receptionist.

"Damn…" he stood up and stretched. He was frustrated.

The phone rang and after a moment of silence, she pointed toward the double glass doors framed in brass. Upon entering, there was another receptionist.

"Oh my…" before he could sigh.

"He is expecting you. The door on the left, she directed them. The doors automatically opened as they approached. The American voice filled the huge office; the English-speaking man faced the bay window that overlooked Seoul.

Mugumbi had never seen a city line from this view. They stood and waited as this big office consumed their little bodies. The fish tank appeared to be a section out of the Pacific Ocean. The ugliest deepwater fish-man has ever seen. Their teeth looked mangled outside of their mouths. They looked dangerous and exotic at the same time.

The voice spoke from behind the chair. "I caught twenty of them myself. The others were flown in from different parts of the world. He continued his conversation on the phone.

"Yes, not a problem, how about I fly into D.C. next month, say the 15th of April, at the Pentagon at 8:30 sharp." He paused. His chair turned around. It was Na Min, Mugumbi stopped sweating immediately, but he kept his composure.

His cotton and rayon shirt was neatly pressed. The cuff links sparkled. The skinny knotted cream-colored tie was neatly pressed up to his Adam's apple. The gray pin-striped suit looked expensive. The desk had a calendar that sat in the middle, neatly arranged papers, and a miniature golf bag that was an ink pen holder. The miniature bar was to the left and a small conference table to the right, in the far corner stood a coat rack that hung one coat.

Na Min held the phone away from his mouth. He gestured with his finger, "One moment." He turned the chair back towards the skyline. "See you then sir." The conversation ended.

He turned back around to face them both. He leaned forward resting his elbows on the desk. He looked Mugumbi up and down, placing his hands beneath his chin. He sighed. "Please have a seat." He told them. Bo translated.

He twisted his head with his left hand. He showed a doubtful look on his face. Finally, he held his hands in front of him.

"OK listen, you are not hired yet. However, you have six months to learn enough Korean to be able to communicate with me." Bo can be heard translating.

"Second, you will have classes to help you. I will get you a passport, and a work visa. That's if you are hired. For right now, you are considered the help, and only help."

He stood and walked over to the window. He turned around on the back of the left heel of his shoe. The late 70's designed pants flared at the bottom. A neatly trimmed beard and a shaggy hairstyle, "Drinks?"

They both looked at each other, Bo translated.

"Yes."

The atmosphere of the office was calm with the jazz tunes in the background. The ice chattered the glass, the Gin poured smoothly. "Yes." He sipped. "Now at all times, you will have contact with me through Bo. The faster you learn the language." He paused. "Matter of fact, English also, the faster the better." He placed his drink down on the desk next to the Rolodex and ink pen holder. "What we discuss is never, never to be spoken outside of us." He folded his arms, "Never." He repeated.

Mugumbi looked at Bo as he pointed his index finger, and translated word for word. He nodded his head with a hundred percent comprehension.

"You will be paid bi-weekly in cash for learning the two languages; however, you will work for free." he sipped his Gin. He pulled a scrap sheet of paper and wrote down what he would pay him bi-weekly. "In thirty days, I will be going to D.C. You have thirty days to learn these manuals, if so; I will have your passport ready for you." He looked at them both and scratched his nose. "But for right now, take him to Baru restaurant and put him to work." He sat back in his leather chair and reached for his drink. "Bo, teach him everything he needs to know."

"Yes, I will." He responded with a nod.

Mugumbi's armpits were sweaty. He was nervous, and in need of a job right away, finally, he has one.

"One more thing…" he stood up and walked over to the painting on the wall of a Hwarang. His left index finger pushed a button in the right corner of the frame that made the painting slide to the left. The knob on the safe clicked with every turn to the left… to the right… and then the left. "Damn!" he paused. "Oh, I remember it." He started over. Every two months he felt the need to change his combination. As he gets older and tries to remember it, it gets harder.

The safe opened, he reached in and pulled out a small bundle of won. He counted eight hundred thousand won. "Here, this is for your pocket." He tossed the remaining back into the safe.

Mugumbi held his arms close to his side, wiped his palms on his pants leg before he reached for the won, and without counting it he shoved it deep into his right pocket. "Gamsahabnida."

He was surprised. "Now you see…" he pointed his index finger at him, "…that's what I'm talking about. No matter what, practice a language and eventually, you will speak the language."

Bo translated and they all smiled.

"On your way out, the receptionist will take a photo of you for your passport; from there you will go to the restaurant."

They bowed; Na Min waved his hand in disapproval. He extended his right hand to shake theirs and said their goodbyes.

One year later

The hot steam soaked Mugumbi's clothes. The red-tiled floor with a drain hole was slippery wet. His forehead had a glossy shine from working hard, up to his elbows in a deep sink filled with dishes. The half-filled garbage smelt horrible. The sleeves of his dingy white t-shirt were dark brown from wiping his forehead and nose of sweat.

A cook pushed open the door and yelled, "More plates!"

Mugumbi responded back in Korean, "Plates are ready! I got them right here!" he pulled both hands out of the water and slid the soapsuds off each arm one at a time. He carefully walked across the wet floor as he held his balance. Behind him was a wall of clean pots and plates on the stainless steel counter. He grabbed ten plates and took them out to the kitchen. He felt like a peasant.

"Mugumbi!" the cook yelled for him.

His frustration grew every time he heard his name.

The cook peeked through the door, "You have a visitor."

He snatched a towel to dry his hands, tossed it over his left shoulder, took a whiff of his armpits, "Not bad." He walked out the back door of the restaurant into the potholed alley of garbage bins. The stench of old thrown-away food blanketed his face under early morning dew. He looked at his wristwatch and noticed the sun rising. "Damn, it's 5:30." He spoke under his breath.

Bo stepped out from behind a trash bend smoking a cigarette. The red cherry lit up as he inhaled. The scene spooked him. Before he spoke he looked down the alley to make sure he was alone.

"What's going on?" Mugumbi asked. He removed the towel to dry his sweaty palms and whipped his face and neck.

Bo flicked the cigarette butt to the ground, with the toe of his left shoe, stepped forward, and twisted to put it out. His burnt orange double-breasted suit that cuffed at the bottom.

"Aren't you looking stylish?" Mugumbi said.

Bo's mood remained calm. "Hey, it's time." he paused, looked around. He pulled out a new pack of cigarettes, unwrapped the plastic cellophane that slowly drifted to the ground, "Cigarette?"

Mugumbi used his thumb and index to make sure that he only touches one cigarette.

The cherry blazed as it brightened the dark alley, with smoke in his lungs, he placed the lighter in his coat pocket.

"Na Min wants you to deliver a package. My car is around the corner." He started to walk toward the end of the alley.

"Wait...I left my bag." he ran back into the kitchen. A Filipino had taken his place washing dishes. It startled him at first. He traded his work boots for his own. He grabbed his bag and headed out the back door.

"Listen, these are the directions, this is the package and some pocket money." Bo pulled out of the alley onto the one way. "I'm taking you to the subway. Under no circumstances, will you let this package out of your site." He made a right turn and looked in his rearview mirror.

"This is a photo of your contact. Call me once you have dropped the package off, any questions?"Bo looked in his rearview to make sure they were not being followed.

He frowned and shook his head, "No."

"Take this with you…" he reached behind the passenger seat and grabbed a brown paper bag. "…it's a .38 snub-nose revolver, go ahead open it up and take it out. Here are the bullets."

Mugumbi began to load the bullets with his towel to make sure his fingerprints weren't on them. He sighed. They pulled over at the corner store. He reached for the gun, "I'll load it, go in and get some cigarettes." He pulled the car around the side of the store to load the gun.

When he returned to the car he looked nervous.

"Hey… this is nothing, just a little easy work. Just don't let the package out of your site." He pulled up to the subway, "Call me if you have any questions." They shook hands.

He took two steps at a time down to the subway platform. He stopped to read the directions. He looked to his left and then his right. All the signs were written in Korean. He compared it to his directions and figured out what train to take.

"This way." he paid for his train ticket.

The early morning crowd carried their coffee, tea, and briefcases. They bundled together as the train approached. The streaking sound of the train came to a stop. The crowd pushed and shoved their way on. He kept the package under his left armpit. He noticed some people read novels and newspapers. Several people had their face masks on to keep from spreading germs. He sighed deeply as the train rocked and wobbled its way along the track. He periodically thought of the gun in his back pocket. He looked at the directions. He counted ten more stops. The closer he got. The more nervous he became. He began to pop his bones throughout his body.

"Ding ding." He exited the train and took a deep breath. The platform overlooked the city. The sun was in full bloom. "Taxi…" His Korean was not perfect but he said, "…take me to this address." The taxi driver nodded his head and waved his hand to indicate to get in.

Forty-five minutes had passed and he was awoken by a pothole in the road. He quickly reached for the package and gun. "Where are we?" He looked around and read his directions. He licked his lips and stretched.

"You will be there in five minutes." He held his hand up to show five fingers. He figured his Korean was not that great because of his accent.

The apartment building was seven floors, a clean, decent neighborhood. He noticed the kids yelling and playing in the first apartment. He looked down at his directions. "Apt 505." he sighed and knocked four times, and paused. Then two more times.

A voice oozed from beneath the door before the door slowly opened. The guy had a short military-style haircut, blonde, deep sunken blue eyes. He stared at him from head to toe. He looked European, perhaps German or Russian. His mustache was bushy and smelt like expensive aftershave. "Are you alone?" his Korean was almost perfect to him but he knew he was not born in this part of the world.

Mugumbi looked around, "Yes I'm alone."

"Quickly come in." he stood aside and let him pass. He checked the hallway to make sure. "Did anyone see you come into the building?" he closed the door before he could respond, "Have a seat, relax."

The sound of the locks on the door clicked, snapped, one by one, three of them. He sighed. This guy does some type of drugs he thought.

The apartment had three bedrooms and two bathrooms and looked pretty much unlived in. The wooden floors moaned and cried as he walked to the minibar. The smell of food lingered from the kitchen.

"Is that it?" the European asked.

"I'm Tony, they call me the Dutchman." He gave him a drink.

Mugumbi gave him the package and thought about the photo of the guy he had in his pocket.

"I have something to give you, hold on." He went into the kitchen and opened the package. He looked around into the living room. "So, where are you from?" The Dutchman asked.

"Africa," Mugumbi said.

Tony came out from the kitchen, "I'm from Holland, but I grew up in Pusan."

Mugumbi sized him up. He looked like a muscular fighter, couldn't tell from the loose clothes he had on.

"I'll be right back. I got to get some things from the car that I have to give you." Tony left the apartment.

Mugumbi sighed, he felt uncomfortable. He stood to walk around to get rid of the butterflies. He cracked the door to one of the bedrooms. It was small, clean for a guy he thought. He quickly looked in the second bedroom. His eyes opened wide. It was covered in plastic, even the ceiling. He quickly closed the door. That room gave him the chills. He walked across the painful-sounding wooden floor to the kitchen. The opened package on the counter had a note. His eyes opened, it was in Korean, but it didn't make sense. He heard a door close in the hallway of

194

the apartment building. He read the note one more time and figured it out. His heart pounded in his chest as he headed to exit the apartment.

Tony opened the door, "Hey sorry it took me a while." He gave him an envelope with some money and asked him to help him move something from the darkroom covered in plastic.

He sighed and felt like maybe he was just jittery. Tony walked in first and opened the door to the closet. "Yeah, I have to take this to my friend. He was relieved when he found out he was moving photography equipment. He sighed, but the note.

"Wait…" he told him as he held up one end of a heavy generator. Tony walked behind him to clear their path. The razor-sharp piano string was tossed around Mugumbi's neck. They struggled hard and violently. He flipped him over his shoulder and slammed his body to the floor. The sound of plastic raddled loudly. He punched him and kicked him in the ribs. Tony pulled the piano wire tighter and pulled him to the floor. Mugumbi broke loose and kicked him again in the head.

Tony pulled a knife and cut him across the chest, leaving a bleeding wound. Another slice on his upper arm, blood fell on the plastic as he charged him with the knife over his head.

He tried to reason with him, but he only responded with rage in his face. They both fell backward as he reached for the .38 and shot him in the chest. He slumped on top of him. He pushed him to the side and rolled onto his back. He couldn't believe all of this. He cleaned the gun and dropped it. He pocketed the money and ran into the kitchen to read the note again.

"Damn!" he first read the note, it did not make sense, it read to kill him and get rid of his body. He sighed and knew he had to quickly get out of the building. He grabbed a shirt from the other room to cover the wounds and blood. He opened the door just enough. He walked calmly but not unnoticed, but he escaped.